The Return of Painting,

The Pearl,

and Orion

A   T R I L O G Y

by Leslie Scalapino

NORTH POINT PRESS
San Francisco 1991

Parts of this book have appeared in *Avec, Big Allis, Bombay Gin, Conjunctions, Notus, Paper Air, Poetics Journal, Scarlet, Temblor*, and a DIA Arts Foundation publication.

A piece from "The Pearl" appeared in the anthology *Under a Single Moon*.

The title "The Return of Painting" is taken from a statement by Julian Schnabel.

Library of Congress Cataloging-in-Publication Data

Scalapino, Leslie
    The return of painting; The pearl; and Orion : a
trilogy / by   Leslie Scalapino.
        p.   cm.
    I. Title.   II. Title: Return of painting.   III. Title:
Pearl.   IV. Title: Orion.
PS3569.C25R48   1991
813'.54—dc20   90-49883

Contents

THE RETURN OF PAINTING

3

THE PEARL

85

ORION

149

The Return of Painting,

The Pearl,

and Orion

A   T R I L O G Y

The Return of Painting

A Novel

People going to small shops, on a street one over that runs parallel, so that it is not facing them. There is clement weather which is not varying in this place though the day and the night are not the same. The young person living there, having an intense tortured as if tearing in half pain in the middle, waking lying asleep, though this had only occurred this one time. The day and the night being free of the one person, who hadn't had this tortured sharp pain as if to tear her in half except this one time, the man lying waking staying gently with her during it through the soft darkness and then ending in the warm balmy day with the people around who go down the street.

The physical pain that was only the one time in the night ending in the light weather when early day had come was inexpressible. The young woman took no drug to end it and lay all day without it and in the heavenly physically light day of early or afternoon. She could not have a thought. Or, having a thought with no drug and now no pain, in the blissful physical day in which the thought did not move. There were no animals around, except for the people who go down the street.

The pain was simple. The doctor did not want to treat her, fearing it was serious and might be trouble to her who was the doctor. It was eventually treated but did not occur inexpressively as it had again.

———

She had a job which was simple, for money. The job was waiting on guests at the table of a blind ninety-six-year-old woman who was astonishingly perceptive though wealthy from birth. Money from birth is a lack. The young woman had to stay over night, away from home. Waking in the morning to wait on the very old blind woman, only she could see the view, bright blue from their high building among other high buildings and the Bay. Not wearing a uniform, she went down and bought the newspaper at the Mark Hopkins Hotel.

There is no low work, but the people recognized the young woman who was not so young, thirty-five, and her function. Wearing her ordinary clothes, she walked into the high-ceiled Mark Hopkins Hotel to a shop in the arcade to buy a newspaper in the heavenly morning. Her job was simple, she had no animosity and liked the blind very old woman. Limousines pulled up to the curb at the street and the young woman returned to her going toward the doorman at the high building in front of the Bay.

The old woman bathed, very white skin, which she liked to do herself, standing with someone averted near-by. One breast was missing but it did not matter in regard to her being beautiful. Dressing her, she wore a wide hat and long gloves and a silk dress which is blue.

A woman similarly very aged wealthy from birth lived downstairs, who had been deserted. The very old woman's chauffeur had run away with the whiskey and silver. Other servants refused to work for her, so then she was left literally with chocolates as someone's gift and was then sent down a sandwich by the blind other old woman wealthy from birth who, nevertheless, had a man take it to her instead of the young woman who worked for her.

An old man died, told to the very old woman by phone, in the high building by other high buildings and the Bay but which was open and blue.

She wept, frightened.

There was a vacant space where the employer was taken somewhere by others one day. The young woman walking down the hills into China Town alone with the Bay visible and down Columbus Avenue.

In the night, the job of the young woman was to read her a book. The aged woman barely able to stay awake was excited by the story of people she actually knew who were on the wall in pictures. The White Russians who were the last to leave whom no one would accept were drifting in a ship in the middle of the sea. They were thrown overboard when they died of typhoid, the ship drifting in the blue sea. The old woman sleeping in the very late darkness as it was read while the young woman, really thirty-five, followed the shallow innocent reactionaries some of whom died.

Getting up to have coffee alone in the high building among the other high buildings and the street below down to the Bay. And waiting for the very old woman to wake.

This woman really reminded her of someone else, though the other person was not wealthy from birth, which makes a difference because people as that regard themselves as special which is nothing. Though the old-woman-now really was special in some which were other ways.

She died a month from then.

The first other one was similarly dainty and regal and astonishingly perceptive which was in her skin. Centered. Standing with cheroot in mouth by railing of ship.

In port, old sitting in cart surrounded by beggars, had not been wealthy from birth or anything of that sort. She did not seem to be old, though she always was to that memory.

When this other woman old then was killed in an accident, she said to her son beforehand when he came to the door which was opened for him, "I thought you were the archangel come to get me." The young woman imagined the accident and the coffin while it was occurring before she knew about it. Afterwards, she dreamed the old one was riding slowly up a hill seen sideways not turning without speaking. And that was now a long time ago, it must be given up.

The couple stood by the sea on the boardwalk in hot weather when all the people come out to walk or stand. Hundreds stand leaning on the sea wall along the curve which extends on the sea rim of the city. The couple looked over the sea wall seeing rats beginning to mass and to scamper and fight on the rocks. There is no beach.

They were not to open their doors onto their balcony at the hotel.

In another city — there is no childhood, there is no such thing — crowds of family and workers could be seen from above from a bus winding through the streets. The shops were open. People worked in light hectic work with great effort which did not cease in the day. Millions of people can be seen from outside in the one-side-open shops and houses.

This did not remind the young woman not-so-young, because it was the same. Beggars or people starving lying in garbage, fruit rotting rinds a foot deep in the street, though that was not happening now. A starving man lying holding out his cup to her though he did not care. In port, they had been walking. A ship's mate, a grown man, walking slowly ahead of her, looking back as if to watch out for her who was a little girl.

Pigs were embedded in lily bogs, and large cattle were also. The green lily pads were enormous, and the bogs occurred here and there in the city.

There is no childhood – people are the same. Or they're not at all the same.

Very beautiful flowers, what is that. Anemones, which are animals. The man and woman fuck though he doesn't this time for some reason of his own or does, but he sucks her with her legs parted so that she comes but he does not know it.

They go down the street. Are out. He does not know she has come that way.

China Basin, where is that. All trucks going in the streets, except for the young woman's car. The trucks honk at her when she is slow or does not know where to turn among warehouses so that the man who's a grown man in one of the trucks doesn't know what turn she's going to make. Not anemones, which are mature men standing with their legs planted apart, one walking to the cab of his truck after the young woman asked him for directions, and he'd said them.

The man, of the couple, perhaps did not come on that time – anemones – and she had when he had sucked between her legs with her legs parted. The mature grown man didn't know she had then.

Some other time, winding by the rim of the blue heavenly Bay in the car – there is no childhood.

Other men in the neighborhood where the illness becomes noticeable having had this time to come up to the surface. The bathhouses had been open for awhile and then that had changed, which was sometime ago. And the sores that are the indications of the illness which will lead to that person's dying look obvious on some men walking in the neighborhood, who are out.

On many people. Other men flock in the street dressed in leather flooding into the middle of 17th Street where there is a funeral parlor. Driving, they're seen at a distance, a crowd, open, congregated but in front of the funeral parlor.

More of them – it's not old age, that isn't it – in the depression of the young person-fragile-man, or his concentration, the young woman hailing some fragile-man she knows from a distance crossing at a light. Other grown mature person tough who's lost muscular control, in wheel chair, takes time fighting. His ashes thrown or scattered on the yard of a center.

Line of people, or crowd clothed in leather, flooding out when a person comes around the corner in a car on the open very clear street.

Blind very old acute woman, before has her listen to tape of someone saying cradling maggot-eaten dying person in the arms to not have that one individual die on the street – there is no childhood, there's no such thing – retrieving the maggot-eaten person from the street and wanting "the babies, the little babies" to live who had not been born yet listened to on the tape in the high building which is in front of the open blue Bay. Active.

Whose.

Another man says he does not mind and does not the decomposing, beautiful decomposing. Holding to lift the tough mature unspeaking person who'd lost control, shit from that sick man on the young man if it may be visible open. The young man wanting to be alive, that's all there is – there is no childhood.

Couple go, driving to border. Just sea is the line along which they're going. They fuck. Woman does not fuck at first. She sucked on the man in a tent on the sand by the ocean. The young man holds back, trying to, lying down on back in front of her – and comes, she knew that he did then and later.

Other first old woman had died in accident – when young woman was really a young woman. She'd said the archangel was coming to get her, out of nowhere, going out the door putting a radio into the young woman's hands – "Here, you have this." Old woman from out of car slid or floated alone along the highway but was dead.

A woman with her, younger but not so young, out of the car lived. Strangers sat with this one. It was raining. They held a coat over the living woman.

The young woman at a different time not the one in the car had no money or job. Money is nothing. Jobs are nothing, days, open, walking down the street though she was in misery at that time from something else. From having been with a man, which now with that person gone was extreme pain. From no money, she tried to sleep. In the darkness, she remembered the one thing there was to eat there, an orange. In the soft darkness alone in bed, coming back to it with it, peeling the orange its odor scent in the dark – eating it, eating – and then the physically light day without the orange's scent. She was very thin – the orange was the same as her the person. Regardless of no job.

People in bar with maroon or orange hair. Very blissful bar or setting. Whether there was or whatever they had been drinking, only a little. The people the same as them.

Before, she'd had an extreme surface which came from being with someone and him now being gone. Going out for a walk, because she felt very sick and had to go out, people walking along – went further and further past them, up the Avenue until stopping to drink a juice. She sat at the juice stand. The people serving her there were suspicious wanting her to move on from her appearance. She was not able to continue. Realizing she was really physically sick and it was simple.

She had a transitory illness – not from him – the same as them. But what had happened in the other situation was there.

The men dying of the other illness, not identifying with that. She met a man who had a very serene identity not identifying with it. The couple went to Guerrero Negro. Coming there in the evening, there was a sand storm. Sand floated across the roads, the couple coming into the poverty-stricken miners' liquor store where those men waited in line to buy liquor – the same as them.

In the tent on that time, of her not fucking the young man, when she sucked on him with him lying on his back in front of her then.

When she worked for the blind very old woman the job was to wait on her at table with the very wealthy visitors not as an extreme surface but as open clear. Without animosity, which was hard for her to do – though they may be innocent or shallow. Or may not be those, though wealthy from birth.

She did this – she really did.

Going to the ink corporation that was for some work, a surface that was in connection with a job of hers so an action, driving winding among the warehouses by the blue open rim. Going to that ink corporation, and the color of the ink having to be exactly the same – which is impossible – whether it's an action. The men dying of the other illness, not identifying with that.

Being in the public bus as it's driving on the street that runs parallel to where they used to live but moved, and then turns left the bus going down, toward the blue Bay – which is extremely silly. So it's coming up against being silly. Boy drives car with girl, and woman who was then young woman, and older mature man away from the funeral afterwards so that it's only an action. That being what they (they) are attempting, that it be only an action.

Boy was driving just after the funeral on New Year's Eve so it was at night for many miles at first along the ocean, the highway all along the way with many police in cars and on motorcycles. The boy chatted with the girl in the dark front seat exchanging, when the young woman and the older man in the back seat of the car. The boy is speeding very fast, received a ticket from a cop who stops them and looks surprised and questioningly into the back seat at the older unspeaking man.

The boy began to speed again – this is impossible because it was in the past, it must be given up – after the funeral and receives a second ticket from a cop who're catching people.

The mature grown man didn't say anything, the boy who's driving received a third ticket from a cop at night – impossible because it's in the past.

Regardless of the funeral – though it was related to that.

Impossible because it's in the past – and dependent on the older unspeaking man for it to be only an action – regardless of him not or refusing to stop the boy from speeding. In the cop, just that one, looking questioningly into the back seat at the older man. As writing.

That's the only thing that's important, writing.

Reading, the rhino is shot but from appearing in the high grass showing, trotting into the shallow boulder filled stream in front of the humans of whom it is unaware. And the bullet squeezed off with the *whonk* of it and, from his trot, he seemed to explode forward – so that it seems to be the same as this. Someone else's writing. With a whooshing snort he smashed ahead, but lying in high grass, somewhere in there behind some bushes – they hear a deep moaning sort of groan and a blood-choked sigh and go forward to it slowly joking whisperingly, the writer of that who the rest of the time is reading having said seeing it trotting in the grass, "I'll bust the son-of-a-bitch." The rhino was lying on its side, dead.

The writer of that – which the young woman is reading – having been reading, himself, while on the trip.

Write. The somewhat older woman who lived though having slid or floated out of the car and lying in the rain. Her fingernails from the moment presumably of the accident lose their moon lines registering the shock to her light body which return later. She had not been wealthy from birth having the opposite of that circumstance – and not identifying with it as identity. The leathery transparent old rhino being busted in high grass light as the young-then, of that somewhat older, woman standing in the boiling sun earlier on a railway platform providing shade by casting a shadow on the young woman who was a little girl, beggars on the platform as the girl leaned over vomiting in the sun – but not identity.

Seeing a film in which appears unexpectedly, innocently, mature tough grown man whom she (this person now) recognizes and who is, in the film, exactly the same age as the young woman not-quite-so-young seeing the film. He was angry in the film then speaking moving in a crowd which pushes up to him their enraged, on the screen in front of the audience. Who'd been in the dark back seat of the car driving up the coast after the funeral. (Who's also her father.)

Not identity of her – and it is. Which is just amazing.

Going is like playing badminton or some ball game in the clear open day afternoon crossing the light intersection hailing an in that case fragile-man who's crossing at a different side or corner of people fanning out in the street. And with an open space. In the area of that illness, and – writing is all that's important.

Clement weather, and almost the same at night.

Man bursts in at door of bar, seeing his friends who'd deserted him he says at some place, and it was because he was really utterly drunk, and floats by their table when they say there's another person he knows seated down the bar. It is a soft open night outside. He takes a hold of the wrong person's head turning it toward them saying it's not him. While the man whose head it isn't, is seated two down from the man whose head is in his hands – and the bartender said as he's going to veer back to the table where they were for him to keep going to the door.

That man sleeping three nights on the street in that week – where people live is nothing. They were walking laughing trying to curb him putting his hand through a broken glass in one bar as they're going down the sidewalk to leave the bar with him in the heavenly dark night along cafés and bars.

There's an open space.

Just turning around the freeway underpinnings in the small old car but fast as was needed onto the overpass by the high buildings and the Bay in the dark. The young woman, and lots of time spent doing that and not doing anything else.

———————

Living woman who'd been busted out of car and slid on highway – earlier as light young flesh woman running to catch a subway. Entering the subway door, she fell flat on her face on the floor of the car which is very funny to her the other people in the car turning away as custom to not see this.

Didn't do anything else for awhile.

Old first woman, who died in accident, did hula many nights for the children, who were in her family. They'd get to request this before sleep. The hula in her heavy corset.

But not that identity of the circumstance.

A huge white barn owl sailed up to window of the two men one the man who'd been sucked on in tent, seated discussing what they should do, they said that made them decide, and then it flew or floated off among the warehouses low going leisurely.

In the film Bobby Seale recorded older seated relaxed said they'd had to figure out some way to get money for guns. Just got the idea and began selling Mao's red book of sayings at Sather Gate, sold at 2 dollars after buying them for 25 cents. We hadn't even read them yet – he cracked up laughing, didn't read it until selling them maybe for two months and did get some shotguns and a few guns. This is brilliant.

Reading afterwards, literally.

The young but mature woman drove in the car for a few hours in the usually clement weather which is the same, the weather becoming intensely penetratingly amazingly cold then. There was no heat in her car. She wore a thin jacket, an almost tissue thin dress, and finding a thin blanket in the back wrapped it on herself. Stopping standing then to get gas on a hill with the freezing wind cutting through. Men standing around her putting gas in their trucks, they were wearing heavy jackets as she clung wrapped in the thin blanket entirely invaded and cut through by the freezing. One man said to the other standing on the hill, why is it so cold.

She knew she could die, that she would. Reaching home in the cold not able to open the door, her hands had become too cold and couldn't turn the key. It was not just frightening. Write. Her hand turned the key. Inside the house was cold, not as cold as outside. Her bones had been reached by the wind. Her entire flesh invaded pervaded, she lay in the bed under the covers she constructed and then the body beginning to violently shake. The flesh like-a-grapefruit woman slept in the night as if she were sealed – the thin blanket in the car had saved her – the next morning reading the newspaper in her robe and slippers and many bums froze on the street. Living people interviewed who'd wrapped themselves in garbage bags, a woman saying she is waiting to be taken away by her Lord in general. Many bums remaining, rounded up taken away out of the weather.

The pervaded flesh of a man walking up the street one day. And to have to know that – which is silly, coming up against being silly. He is, they are.

Out driving but on the bridge over the Bay and when getting to ramps or overpasses a car is on its roof burning like a flare or torch.

Driving coming around the corner to corner where there are prostitutes always standing and walking, trucks that are junk wrecks here and there on the street, man on bicycle is stopped negotiating with one of the women. Many trucks rumbling by on the street. It is an open clear space.

Whether the person or is there which is silly. In the blue blissful day.

An otter ran across the sand, it was the size of a large dog sleek dark – feeling is nothing, it is not feeling. It ran into the ocean, seen.

Such hot weather, driving, saw cars and vans, and girls in a tiny yard at the intersection playing in the water sprinkler so their breasts and nipples, hair in ringlets, were wet – and stylized wrestling or something utterly incredible with a sole adolescent boy in front of the people in the cars and vans – their.

In the very hot weather – here. Actions are nothing – this is impossible. Have used them up – and writing isn't anything. The older man, very sick in the hospital in the crisis – and not stylized or is, loved, and geared to this.

Geared to this – writing.

Sept. 21 – 102°F, Oct. 5, 1987

14

The man sitting up over the corpse as a vigil, is arising from-him not having money, though it is done with care for someone passing away. And not from lack of money which may be but doesn't matter in the person who died. It is the culture expressing itself in dance, there being that which is beautiful and not related to dying.

It here the culture isn't related to lack of money or to there being that. So the two things coming together is too much. It's too much to float between the two or to be violently rushed into the culture. Unbearable to try. But which people who are poor do also in the area of junk wrecks on the street and then the people entirely separately going to the dance. May.

Some people can't stand it. Not the man sitting up all night in the hours and the others not doing that in the vigil over the body which had died of the illness. It is too much to bear the contradiction. Standing in the dark at the filling station, the young woman, to put in the dollar's worth of gas in the other person's car which they could very well do as filling it, when it should be more.

The older man having a bad infection, the bloody fluid drained from his side – intense pain, screaming – though he gets better. It's not that of money. The dancers do modern expression, and some wore ballet toe shoes in the same dance – which is what it was about.

It doesn't matter. The crisis doesn't or always doing that that it is that though it has worn everyone out. It was clear open anyway – whether it was unbearable in its contradiction also. Whether there's a dollar's worth of gas in the car and could be filled and should be so as not to run out. And always having that kind of situation or behavior, of the gas in the car not enough to go far. On her part. And theirs.

———————

To have violated or going against the procedures of the novel – by doing them.

The otter dark sleek – as large as a dog with sleek legs running across the sand, is the contradiction also. It's being some other animal does not stop that. Or not more so but as much. And very open clear, so that there is no doubt.

Some dancers in the past, many a whole varied troop so that there were a variety of scenes which could go on at the same time in front of everyone, dived into the mountain of dirt on the stage swimming madly – some seeming to drown and others swimming to save them madly.

The dancers in another night walked or dined or anything on the stage in a pervasive surface pool of water, not swimming or drowning – but moving in it doing whatever, so that it was the same as the dirt. There was no dirt then. Which is the contradiction, and writing isn't anything, as is the otter. Geared in that – them.

She's given too much pain-killer at some point – drug – and realizes few people care about each other. She feels or knows they do not care about her – though he does. She does or they do. What does it that matter anyway. Ever. And not as a negative or frightening thing – though it is frightening. Others at other times or periods not frightened by it. And so much over something small. Which is incredible.

Go out for a walk – to the market – sunlight light a little tiny white bird with some kind of orange bill peeped in the gutter; then flies back down again on the walk – peeping in front of her. Not moving – for feeling is nothing – then flies away.

Melon, such a wonderful melon served to two by others one evening.

Open utter fear. So what, that is what everyone may or will – feel – as surface. A dance another one in the past, going on for hours, many people on the stage in unfolding scenes. A man swimming in a blue porthole. Lines of trees floated by in the spectacle when the performers moved the other way than the trees, the most beautiful thing. And that as acting. Out. Public.

In that would be the only way to know – which is extremely silly.

This is not fear – and it is in the past. Not like this.

Film of samurai—remembered, though it isn't this—on hill in wind flags flapping violently, and them planted in seats overlooking the battle when many of samurai or attendants are shot, and are not to move.

(though they win from this)

Another dance or theater, small scenes in different spots visible from the viewers (there is no stage) being above. People dining or going to sleep, the unfolding of the world war in these scenes seen. A Japanese general at the line of performers at the head of it shouting. In just that acting—not this. Someone else's acting. Sensation does not matter, it is not sensation—theirs. No derivation.

A Novel II (a separate novel)

That other was in a theater, not writing. And not event in life.

Remembering – so it's a long time ago, is nothing – looking at a fat cigar-smoking lolling man on a small boat the young girl with another girl who're white standing while he's saying vile things to them – from no event. The white piggish gesticulating man referring to the group of a man who's black bent over at the side of the small boat, who steered the boat. Bullying the young girls with a wave of hate. Not having seen them before. They were on a river. The black man on the boat was looking at him slightly averting his own face.

The girls were averting their frames.

Those really young girls had danced – there's no connection – with two black men who were returning students on the ship; there was a ship's dance, the ship divided into classes – so no one else would dance – in the day, next, some huge gross Afrikaner women slammed them against the wall in the hallway when they found a store on the deck of the class above. The Indian women and daughters never emerged from the boiling hot cabins below deck and the girls strolled on the deck in the Indian Ocean.

A space and at the same time.

A cadet ship's mate came down to their hot small cabin, when they'd just showered were wrapped in towels – and wanted to talk to the girls saying something and the chain on the door of the cabin, him chatting then with the somewhat older man and woman who were young on the deck.

The ship stopping at different ports – some Indian women had smallpox on it, getting into an ambulance at the dock of one port, the other passengers not allowed to disembark – only when they were leaving to go to their own town, or the stevedores coming on and off in lines on the ship.

And no connection to those things, which there isn't.

The students there were many on the ship in the third class having gone to prison then – some – years in prison, reading, and then coming out and in action.

To repeat the same event, written – and to repeat it in the same way in writing always.

She'd before had too much pain-killer, barely getting home and diving for the bed grabbing her notebook in one hand and the pen in the other and slid into the bed. She wrote a paragraph of this – with her head unable to lift from the pillow in that instance. There is no relation.

Go out for a walk – and saw an old man coming forward recognized from him living near-by and he was now very old and white looking madly out of the corner of his eyes – and at her then. Blossoms to one side of him, the sky half evening – then when walking – dark blue and a half moon in it. The cars bumper to bumper in the Avenue, a girl seated on the bench of the bus stop in a light shirt lime green and lime green socks and black shoes, holding a bouquet of flowers with the floral paper around the long stems – a dark sunset behind her followed by the dark blue night and half moon in it.

Sitting – saying

working at a swimming pool, pulling a man out that day – to resuscitate him from a heartattack – a man having died from that being resuscitated by the person speaking, a week ago. The second man was carried out under a mask in an ambulance and

a person hearing this, who was sitting in a back yard with others, going home, meeting a man living across the hall who comes out saying to guess what happened to him. He thought he was having a heartattack being young while swimming, and was resuscitated and carried from there

the man having thought he was having a heart attack at different times from being upset

A dance seen – in a theater – the dancers acted as if their limbs were screwed on backwards so it was a view of air that a person doesn't see. They were in light shorts orange and green undershirt-like tops – flesh – many of them, a group all being young, skipping, frolicking.

– grown man seen on the street going to work in dusty suit flimsy grueling poor of waiter or something less in incredible circumstance (others in the same circumstance fanning out across the street) of repression, his face still, depressed and sensitive in situation of young girls and somewhat older woman but young who's had them get on the bus and go into city on it in the very early morning – and this is a long time ago. This method repeated – there is no novel. The young-then woman has them get on the bus at the airport, though they're not supposed to – many, city, denied visas – and go in to it in the early dawn for that reason.

The earlier writing having done its purpose – which had been to keep the older man alive. Who's loved.

Driving in the marsh area of the Bay in cars bumper to bumper with round moon standing in the light blue evening. The woman is not thinking, the light blue water by and under the bridge ahead is the same as the sky.

Having zoomed away from the hundred year old woman in the light blue evening – when there're cars bumper to bumper – and the very old woman had been lying curled on her bed having wet it incredibly aged in the convalescent home as light open. Struggling and suffering to continue to act – now.

Getting very tired and struggling not to go to sleep sitting in the chair working and swimming back into sleep having driven in the dark blue night to here – and finally getting up from the chair and sleeping for many hours. That is nothing.

During the day – walking back home one day as cars stream up the street that crosses. This person was coming from an area of shops – nothing. Things there are minute only. And was in the light day. Stemming from the minute area, and alone, that person. People out. There was not time to have been coming from it.

Someone else saying something – only in that. From anyone – but actually spoken by them.

Young flesh man – in the past – having driven to the spiraled parking structure looked up seeing rows of hundreds of hooded police lining the spirals. The young man went off in the car parking elsewhere. He came back walking to crowds blocking a center ordered to disperse, the lines of police ran at them clubbing the people in the crowd violently, really and without stopping. It's from someone else – he says this – spoken to this person. He they scattered up the block the police chasing them which were thousands of people there, but the police ranks had to thin out chasing them a few blocks – so they'd run around the block and return grouping again, but were driven off of course. Burning of cars on the outskirts. Many people badly hurt by the police clubbing them. And there's no relation to that.

The couple drive in the desert and see the dehydrated corpses of cattle which are put on sticks – their by the side of the road – as not to go at night. There is not a novel.

To have to really not be valued – or oneself.

As the person being nothing, in that Ronald Reagan (so it's not in the future) as the old aged apparently formed by Nancy as if light dancers in shorts orange and in green tops skipping (their) frolicking – and no connection which there isn't to them those dancers really, in grueling repression of circumstance.

———————

Dining or something, the couples though there more men, are rudely insolent to the young woman who is foreign to them – visiting – a woman who is foreign to her snubs her in the table conversation and with affected and dominated manner.

The couple are seen then – by these people – without any clothes, lying on each other. The pink or rosish tip of the man's stem – the pink long slender stem pointed out – is not in the young woman.

The young man's stem is pointed out – he has an erection though it is not in her yet with him sitting up bending toward her, him innocently unexpectedly, though having no interest in them. The flower opens. Though it is not them.

He enters with his member with a pinkish long tip going into her – and then drawn out, for some ways. And when the man's withdrawn and a space between them. In that time. The woman is lying in front of him, and it is out and with him attentive alert.

The man entered again. He pulls out his penis, then not lying on each other and without any other contact – but his pinkish stem entering her (from his kneeling) and only that doing that.

So that he comes.

She meets them out – uninvited – unavoidably, with others, and they will not speak to her. Of the trussed-up in the sex clothes insolent class-ridden people. Which is really so.

The man who is not like them, with the long stem pinkish unclothed in front of him – and not in her yet. Then putting it in to her.

On a time when she comes from it. These people are out, they always snub the others who are visitors. For those who aren't, in that manner that is class-ridden.

Mature large bull-man rutting but who is not at all one of these. Those who are foreign having the attitude of great restraint and repression the men and women the man's pinkish tip stem unclothed and him making sounds – who's not like them – out. People are in public, on the street.

The mature large bull-man with his stem extended – who's out some time, legs planted apart – coming when rutting but which is not theirs who're foreign. Not that culture. Either.

The mature large bull-man puts his stem in to her.

Before when she'd had to get over knowing someone who was weak and cruel so that she was in extreme pain she fell asleep having a dream in which a man whom she knew but with whom she'd never lain did so to her. This man being usually repressed or seeming so was with the very same manner which appeared repressed joking with her to tell her something to divert her from the pain of the other thing and his stem very far in her. People came into the room so he had to withdraw his penis. He joked with her then still leaning over her but in a manner erotic from being lightly really profoundly intellec-tual – which had been when his stem was far in and pulling out, not in the separation between them when the people interfered by coming into the room. Though then too. He may have entered her again, pulling his stem out again from the people being there – coming in.

The mature large bull-man jabbing with his long slender pinkish stem out in front of him – and that is not her either. Then pulls it out. He is holding back. Then putting it back in. Which it is. He's out, on the street. Standing with legs apart. Or walking. Them – either.

Comes then. Or not. When he'd pulled it the stem out. She does or he. Or he does not, pulled back with the pink long stem out in front of him.

Come to the house, circling it on foot – the doors locked – go down to a bot-tom door, the person inside not being able to move or get to the door to open it. She gets to it; inside – alone for this time, in excruciating pain – this person getting inside, the other one is weeping very angry and this person not strong enough – not able to be picked up, wild pained – to get in to bed or out of it, either – and as Kerouac for this place.

There's a deer in the yard.

As Kerouac for this place – other young man driving fast in wreck-car other cars beside him fast up a hill on the highway – over the top crest, just over the line of vision from the other cars the car-light-machine loses clutch ends and disintegrates stopped in the middle of four lanes at the top over the hill – why didn't you run, other young man says. Young man sat in car with them whizzing by him – laughs, figure if he's hit he might as well be dead with no car insurance – in the light-car over the top of the hill. Machine-car as only connection to this place and then – also.

Their wanting to stop the peace-conversations Reagan and the other aged (this one isn't really-young) – their syndicate, of a war – other-their foreign-leaders to have the peace conversations which now at this time temporarily thwart this.

It can only be very simply to do it – as Kerouac. The man's pink long slender stem extended and then put in to her – and pulls it out again. As to meet that. Of the situation of the peace-conversations, something, which will surely be broken by them. And is. As to meet that with only that.

Man gives her lift, not known very well – driving night across the long length of the city, him speaking on the way – o it's a long time since she'd met anybody friendly then; and coming gently there is no time to have been at them to the red lights all along the way slows low putting on the gas and went through every red light on the street of the entire city. When he'd slowed at one in gutted out buildings for blocks, there's a poor man out walking with a small cat on a leash and jerking it and the man in the car slows stepping on the gas and goes through the red light there.

III

Flying fish in the blue ocean – the freighter going.

Whales – in the swells or still, already having died (seen from the side of one of the ships) in mid ocean – many, so that they're amongst them. Chugging of the engine – but a deep chugging from the freighter slowing or stopping amidst the blood clouds in swells from the flagged floating bodies of the creatures that are being harpooned. That's occurring. A stowaway is sent in a rowboat from the freighter to the other ship. The stowaway or a whaler who falls out of the rowboat into the high swells of waves – the man who'd fallen from the boat waving but not so as to be picked up by them, which he is.

Lying on the rubber inflated mattress-raft in the dark city apartment – person alone. People calling out who're yelling at night. Who're ordinary people or many many all the way along the street in poor clothes asking for money. One man happened to be given three dimes which were in the pocket of the person who is later lying sleeping deeply on the rubber mattress-raft, the man looked so defeated and disappointed by the money that had been given to him.

Before the rubber-raft mattress, her going into the department store – on the mattress raft sleeping deeply as if sunken much later at a different time. From then there had been the crowd of people at the front entrance near subway entrance asking for money, a man on a sled with no legs at the door of the department store – which was merely that with the appearance of cities in it that was really beautiful. Merely commercial as beautiful and could not be done otherwise.

The float mattress raft on the floor – the person in a deep sleep on it as that being the same. But in bitter cold, her face stung by the freezing wind walking at night and people begging on the street in that.

Ordinary other people calling out at night – or yelling things. Heard from the person being on the float mattress raft the flesh machine body stretched out straight.

Balmy – the man crapping squatting by the side as the train goes by seen from his back – lily bogs in the city with small dark pigs floating in them.

But it's bitterly cold – outside, not from lying on the mattress floor raft or people out – which is the same, which is that.

People squatting outside. Or washing.

Seen from riding in the bus – so above, people many all along the street with their backs to the cars and bathing wet with soap delicately from spigots that would be out from a wall many on the street.

Woman crapping on the sidewalk near a restaurant in front of which she lives – out. Living there.

Going into the lobby where the people, who're really chic, or who've been met won't speak to a person who's not important – class-ridden asinine, really destroyed by them.

> who grew up in the forest and emerged from
> it a singer because he had been talking with
> the birds throughout his childhood

Going on the subway which stops and slows – before that on the mattress raft float lying – only shuts down to downtown trains, from a man who's walking on the track obstructing.

Everywhere people around – shivering in the freezing wind. Asking for money.

IV

The taxi goes up today in a gutted block from way downtown to the chic. The person is very tired so that the voices were temporarily induced flooding – which are anger, why anger. Frequently the same – and reaction of anger – which the mattress raft float is the same but not identifiable. That is not anger. The downtown subway trains stopping because a man was walking on the tracks, she runs up out of the subway station to the taxi, that's passing by on the street. It's day. Going back the length of the city that had been crossed into a gutted block rather than downtown, and then in another new taxi again through the entire length of the city and back to downtown. Can't be the means of anything. And a light warm day in winter.

Crazed angry voice but many in people as just what they are – the only thing as being that.

Lying on the mattress raft float is in this – in nights. And is not a means to anything.

This isn't either – not either one. The mattress raft – the person as not important, chic.

Meeting a warm compassionate person – and people around saying they're them so stupid they don't know anything.

Went to a lake that was pale blue with white desert. And read a book there, fierce cattle coming down close to her or they were frightened. For hours by it, two days rugged terrain and in beating sun, sleeping at night alone on the hard metal back in the car. Reading intently by the pure blue water in the beating sun, with the fierce cattle close – in the day. Then getting up from the book when it had been read, relieved.

The person gambling alone, putting nickels in the slot machines in casinos, stopping driving in desert towns – and winning.

No derivation.

Person loses ability to understand – flips out – and that at the age of a child, so that it's irrelevant – and must be given up. Otherwise no one can learn – so they're so stupid.

because they were children

And now there's no connection to them – having been a child then (the person). Nor is that cared about.

Chic brings tears of desperation. They are not that. Coming up to being chic.

The place that is near the Arctic, port, where they had dogs but which had to be silent or the animals didn't live long. They would shoot them. Working. Lightly populated port, and when certain ships came the people kept their dogs in because they would be caught by the sailors. – for eating. Light white place.

Reading intently alone at the pure blue water which was cold in the beating sun with the fierce cattle close by. Standing waist deep in the lake with rock pyramids the person alone – it is the fierce cattle starting and shying or as if to charge – and when it had been read, feeling very relieved.

The setting that's ocean of townspeople getting a dock – to have the catch brought in there. And a man who'd catch a fish, him standing in the water ocean wading the fish to the shore – and with the people looking from it.

An airplane crossing the country where the man in it and as might be, showing not wanting to speak to the other men – who're with him or meeting up passing through the plane and saying not aware of where they're going this time joking – beds of clouds with the light shining on the fields of clouds are under it. The one seated concentrating on his business on work, not through but resting. Him only doing that.

and from being in that chamber
with light on the clouds

The place that the people gamble during the day or get off the bus crossing the clear desert – from elsewhere – and put the nickels in the slot machines. Working there in the towns. Or who don't.

Driving in the clear light desert even if they live there.

Or not living there driving in the clear desert.

There not working except the subways many people as is needed – going through the cars for money. A man would offer to not play a saxophone and the seated rows on either side giving him a little – moving.

The building by the river which changes with the light, though it's a tomb – so it's not really a building floating. Light of evening swallows sparrows and other birds rushing it in flocks in the air. At night lightning showing it in the heat.

Thin man's many men's torso's undressed wrestling alone individually and with dying – to it being at that area in undulation.

Going in the car through the light spring green earth and hours – the hot road, populated – the car bounding.

The building by the river which changes with the light, and people flocking into it – evening dusk with the birds rushing it in waves outside, the people calling out in it, a constriction and wild – mania of calling – and men with rifles having to drag the flock of people from it.

V

The man – he says this – reading in a scene of confusion. The main act was a film shown on the bald head of the author of it and people were milling there so that they couldn't be distinguished from the readers. His turn came. He said to a woman who had come to see him that he couldn't read the writing that was for her, because of being in that confusion. She requested it – and reading it, he saw a man on crutches coming toward him, who fell on his this man's feet. The man who'd been on crutches held onto his feet – another woman hit the fallen man who'd been on the crutches with her purse – was doing that.

A man got a job painting a house with a family of brothers fathers who paint. He was with a brother up on the boiling slate roof to brush out the gutter, the heat coming through their shoes and burning their buttocks, who were dressed in shorts. Down on the ground again he was asked to mix the paint with turpentine – going to the men, after finding a can, to see if the paint is thinned. They paint a side. At lunch the men look for the can to urinate, the man having used their urine instead to thin the paint. He's painting attached to hooks but the hooks are not fastened to the roof very well, asked to get down and a much heavier man gets up carrying paint and slips down swings through the garage door hitting other cans of paint where he hits. He's painting then standing on a beam stepping back to look and another man standing on the other side, the beam flies up, falls painting a stripe.

The people driving on a bridge over a tributary of the bay, where a long fleet of ships is tied which are retired, the steam in heavy rain, and the oil refinery there – the sky light.

A woman reads in a tent where there're many people – others first. Going to the center ring, the crowd had broken off adjourning to a bar there in the tent with their backs turned making a din. She reads. A few people seated on the stairs facing downwards to the tent ring – her reading, of breast-feeding, they concentrated. The few people laugh, the main crowd continuing making the din at the bar.

Solitude.

The people seeing those with very thin chests, some with torsos unclothed – bowed. Those in crowd going a long way on the roads bowing in dust.

A person walking in the freezing countryside in a parka, gloves wool clothes, and no one else being around. Angry voices wrestling in the person as she's concentrating and walking, beside the road in the snow were the marks of a struggle of a bird picking up an animal. The dark glasses of the person freezing over but the glare from the light snow blinding, feet numbing, having to get back to home – then listening to the radio, people to be in from the freezing, children not to be going out to schools.

A woman reading on the radio, and then in the great heat she and a man bicycling by the corn fields a dark sky that seems to be a tornado near where they'd come from, where they're living. Bicycling back because of that, sweating in the heat. A dog chasing them up the road. The siren of the tornado warning whined. At night a strand of lightning singes the building, there in bed in the dark. Turning on the radio to hear which has just been blasted back on, after going off.*

A man has the job sand or fire with solvent blasting or wrenching apart huge bolts or valves that had been in oil drilling or ships so saltwater corroded, low-paid pulling them apart with their hands or shooting solvent on them so they'd be aflame. Old machinists working near-by repairing the bolts or valves, the low-paid would shoot each other with the solvent joking so that the apron of the one would catch on fire briefly, an old machinist would then squirt the solvent suddenly on one the apron aflame, and they'd throw a huge bolt across the room at each other. It is in a bad neighborhood, little children coming to the wire fence looking in at them shouting you old fuck or something to a machinist. A machinist would throw a bolt at the children who'd laugh standing at the fence, from his joke. The man would then be out in the yard on the boiling asphalt, the little children watching him setting aflame a huge corroded pipe with solvent, wiping out the corrosion, in his shorts sweating like a pig.

Two men reading, her seated in the center of the room where there are pillows on a pillow. People around seated, some would not speak out of snob-

*See Jerry Ratch, *Plein-Air*, for fields with crows in them.

bery or being young. And not knowing anyone there, yet a man begins to physically nudge her off the pillow which she would not gracefully give to him and he finally does actually knock her off of it and sit on it. Getting a ride across the bridge with the lights coming from the bay, and the driver saying things are in clubs or groups.

A couple went out on a long strip of huge rocks on the ocean where there was a flock of small sea birds – not gulls – which rose and rushed in the air. But the couple continued climbing and walking on the rock-strip, the birds settling and rising anew in a flock in front of them – rushing in the air light changing at the same time between them in the sky with one cloud.

It took a long time.

The man overseeing or hearing very young men in the airport and on the plane in civilian clothes, short sleeves rolled with cigarette in it to bare their arms. Exhausted, strong – not knowing what time it is or day. Working. Coming from Sinai Peninsula where for months they'd been in the desert in tanks, and on their way to base together.

The person not being able to walk well, in the game park with the mat laid down for her to climb under a fence seeing wild birds start up flocks V's fanning through the air.

The young boys go out together in the woods carrying a .22 walking conversing about one's view that squirrels sleep in the tree tops and begin shooting and shooting. Nothing happens. And then in one shot a squirrel falls down in front of them, the bright red blood splashing around. It's not yet dead. They regret it. On the ground, the eldest shooting it to kill it.

Man climbing stories-up high girder without ropes in the rain – to do something, work – and without any scaffolding on which to climb it. Wrapped around it with his arms and legs.

The old – machinist – throwing the ship's bolts or oil drilling bolt at them through the shop.

And then an other man standing in shorts on the hot asphalt outside to shoot the huge pipe with solvent that had been corroded.

Having torn the huge corroded valves apart with their hands, two men pulling on the same part or not being able to do this.

Shooting it – the small children watching, as him sweating like a pig working.

Which is not slipping on a banana peel though working on the corroded huge pipe. That had been in the sea.

And shooting the solvent – standing.

Or doing so – and the person working concentrating and overseen by them watching.

Which doesn't have anything to do with that.

Shooting the pipe with the solvent.

People getting down and jack-hammering in the street, trenches having been cut so that there're long wedges cut in the downtown street and their getting at the pipes of the sewers. Waist-deep digging in the holes.

Had, traveling, light snow that was coming down outside, in New England a happy dream of living in what was Tokyo and, knowing someone was trying to kill me, a part of the dream in trying to hire a person actually known slightly to protect me but who was not responding in this to me. And realizing I was very seldom happy in a free sense of that – living there freely. Happy then.

VI

An earlier dream. Of being killed by a man a hired killer shooting the rifle, into the vertebrae running up a hill on gravel and feeling dying. Completing dying. And very happy. Awaking. Lying astonished.

Not with the characteristics of this person in life – just physically dying in it, and it not a duplicate – and there was simply the other dream later which in the present has similarities to it.

So that it's entirely in the dream. The person in it saying it would be better to die than to be in this terror. And then dying. Something being repressed in great pain in that time. Very simple. Not in this writing – and being only in the dream so that the person's changed.

A man somewhat older got money, seemingly endless hundred dollar bills (given to him) and says I'd always thought I'd die in a ditch like a dog. I said I thought I would too. Not *you*, he says. And he mature tough man could die in a ditch with hundred dollar bills in his pocket. The bills stuffed in his pocket.

Reading something – having lived or been in the city, and now that one's mind has turned to other things – thinking why is this, someone else's book but of a manner one had been in, so difficult. Why isn't it simple. The response is simple. This is simple.*

To have a complete imitation.

Is not it be an imitation, but just that same thing. What is that? A woman receives all the attention and sympathy – sitting weeping – strong – and the other person would not weep, or want to, or does sometimes, having given that sympathy in this other's emotion – and travel

adventure
which is what the weeping person does

*See "Cereal," by Alan Davies.

And to be very calm

                in it (that same thing) and happy

Some guys not most people – who like little boys being in a gang or crowd – so that it was necessary to get into a fight with the main bully like at the end of the comic book. In being beaten by the bully on the beach the weakling has to lift weights at home to come back and beat him up.

The main bully started it. Once he spoke to the woman, and the muscles rippled up his arm. He was going to hit her. Coming from not being their conception of what someone should be as public.

                as I am

It was devastating to write back and forth and have the verbal fight with him. And he continued laughing, with his supporters.

                very happy
                to them
                and just that

It was easy.

                because of that

And not worrying.
Went to the Gulf. It was beautiful.

A man and woman traveled. Thunder clouds come up as they're sitting on the porch and come toward them. There's heavy brief rain. Houses and people in the Gulf towns. A dock going out, into the sea. They drive.

Road runs along so near the ocean of the Gulf right up to it that it is a thin rut between the tall waving grass, no cars, – of others – and the ocean. Driftwood having floated over the rut. Big thunderheads hang in the sky. To Port Arthur which is oil refinery and the blue ocean, the flame shooting up waves around the jet of fire as in the center from the refinery empty center of the town with newspapers blowing past the thirties buildings and to the gas stations and hamburger joints on the outskirts.

A surface where there is something which is light, and which is turned upwards. She was standing on the rim of the crowd who're flocked around the bars of an ape's cage which spat into the crowd and a huge ball of spit drenching her cheek at that far rim. It was spitting over and over, the people congregated and here and there.

In Chicago rim of lake. A tape at a zoo played saying the apes were happy – and the people looked on quietly – while an orangutan with a very long arm, the long red orange arm beat on the door. Monotone of banging. The group of orangutans looked at it quietly.

The other time – the ball of spit hitting the cheek. It was water, the ape had been drinking.

Very happy

Standing at the rim of the crowd – being at the rear when the spit had covered the face, with the people congregated in front of one and scattered.

A person falling. On flesh. Young flesh woman – then – falls off of curb into street and the crowd of passersby, to cross the street, do not look at her from embarrassment out of custom.

> rim of
> crowd then

not the woman falling in the street. Where there was nothing happening.

> or that

The ape – happening to spit – on that one person who was standing who was me in the crowd or was on the outskirts of it.

The woman – walking, some other time.

Life is a pure dream.

Nothing ever goes back. Some other person saying Just go forward.*

Went – getting visas – in the carriage of a three-wheeled scooter up the empty hot wide street past embassies which are spaced-out, trees, people at the gate of one to admit them. Letting them in bowing which is a foreign thing in this place which is also foreign.

*"Just go forward," Philip Whalen.

to that

Being incarcerated very old curled can't move she said I wanted to commit suicide and I didn't know how says weeping I didn't know how have you ever been that low yes and that means that this is what this is.

A man getting on a bus carrying a huge sack of crushed cans he'd collected for a living barely get the garbage through the bus door – spilling the cans, the passengers who're the same as him make minute motion inside of them of beginning to get down and pick up the cans – decide not to move forward – and he does it.

Picks up the cans in the bus moving.

Their not moving.

Going by gutted area.

And the bus continuing.

Sitting – saying

Man he's only fifty then digs up at night the pipes the men from the sewage system had worked on to hook up to the sewage. The person who says this having looked out the window at the sewage men digging in a trench in the sheets of rain. And the man coming home there from work at night digging them up again that night in the rain finds only two pipes are hooked to it. She says that to them the next day so they come back and do it.

How could you know that, they say to her

and she says he dug them up.

A person going out floating with no one around in an inner-tube on a lake far out. Daily, during part of the day and on one time it becoming over-cast. Dark water on which the inner-tube is and fairly dark sky. And the one person there.

––––––––

Go through the green hills in the car. A glutinous wrapped calf dropped from a cow – as a young man drove by before on the curves of the road. It was a pod a glutinous creature which fell out on the ground from her rear, in front of him. Him driving amazed. He said this. By fields of water which comes up to the road.

Some men like little boys jeering openly putting down the person who would speak – who were themselves not with ability – and that person with ability.

Man's tone in speaking, implying jeering, requiring a submissive tone on the person's part – she refuses, in speaking, to do that, that when the muscles rippled up his arm appearing to be going to hit her.

Seated – man jeering scornfully at their ability as not to have that by nature, singling two out in front of everyone who had been the best and worst – and both having to fight verbally, the other men unconcerned seated around them. Those men on the side of the authority.

Having to be this – foolish – thing – which is irrelevant – and makes no sense.

Standing in front of the people who were seated, and those men who were like regressed boys, not having developed, jeering, laughing – mocking openly at the person who had said something – in amongst those who were leaders and were laughing wanting this.

Seeing a film, as it happened, of some sitting in at a lunch counter in a dime store sit-in, the man throwing a milk-shake splashing covering the face of a young man seated, who bows his face. Guided. Is seated.

Boys in crowd who break loose, running – without recourse – and the men beating and clubbing a boy they catch, whether they had been alert guided or not. Seeing it on a film. The men clubbing are of the minority which is the repressive authority.

Guided. Not guided. Not having been guided seated in the class, having done the worst on the test which is foolish, nothing, knowing that and having to fight. Which theirs would be to be that other thing and then supposedly be accepted but to be accepted will never be. To have to be not oneself. Knowing that. Not guided.

Theirs as being the best one and the worst of the group that was being sneered at, but not of those doing the sneering – doing better than all of those – and both of the persons not to have ability which is fine ability or anything at all from the very act of how they'd done the mundane test – he says – and the other men seated going along with this.

To have to be not oneself.

And will be what occurs, seemingly what was going to occur.

The rain came up in the sewers and flooded so the landlady who was in her nineties had her work the pump, them wading in the water in their house.

The pump giving shocks, but the partly deaf landlady doesn't understand her refusal to work it. Or does.* The other goes out for a walk the basements of the houses everywhere are in water. And feels light and happy. It raining.

Hearing the yelps from the house from a man who lives there the landlady had gotten – to wade with the pump. Instead of her.

Hoses coming out of the houses, as she walks.

And no one around – and the river flowing on the street.

The very old landlady cackling and snorting when there are shocks from it – with her the other holding the pump and they're wading in the water. No one around.

They're. The motor going of the pump on a cord in a lake.

And outside, the river everywhere.

The glutinous calf – groups-of-people not communing. As the edge – of that place.

In Chicago rim of lake. Her being locked out of car and her by the blue lake of a warm day in park and near stores.

Buying a book. And reading, by the car – which is locked.

Not learning, but reading.

What is that?

Glutinous pod of calf – which is not that.

And no relation. To itself.

---

* "Here you can't carry this," Margaret Evans. I came home from a trip I was so tired I was pushing my bag with my foot up the street. She was in the yard grabbed it ran up the stairs with it.

I was driving warm day and I saw this trailer-truck cars on it its ramp down and I thought of driving up its ramp – and thought of the man who was on it then just putting a car on, being amazed and shouting get off.

Walking – in the day sky is a half moon, and looking up birds skimmed through the trees.

VII

Picking up the old car it having been repaired, from the garage – and driving, chugging lurching to go home – through the streets a towtruck that is there begins going along side, to get a job.

Having picked up the old car – from being repaired, but that is a long time ago – when driving across town in the car lurching – and a man in a towtruck which begins to go along side it, just from around, began waving to tow the car.

It happening before.

Wave him off.

Coming from the outside, which isn't really.

Set off into the street now where there was no one around – it is a large neighborhood, parallel and to, immense homes – alone – walking in the day, but there's a light for crossing and a man on a bicycle, when there wasn't anyone, rides by out of nowhere and shouts in the ear. Shouts could have been killed walking there.

He shouts in the ear – going by on the bicycle.

At the large street – in a deep and serene peace – and no one around, the ear like a shell. When having been walking.

Walking, driver has the car race forward, as the one walking is in the neighborhood street, and speeds up to cut off that one, to go first – the one almost putting up the finger to give it, to the driver, after. A smirk on the face of a passerby at the one who's been cut off who is there.

A man is on a bicycle not having been seen – rides up to the car, haranguing and shouting that he would have been killed at the driver's turn who hadn't seen him, in affluent – on the neighborhood street, shops, cars bumper to bumper, in the day. The head of the man on the bicycle is in the car window to harangue – and of person who before was walking.

Almost saying well you're not dead.

Woman crossing at intersection moved her hips very slowly sullen, when car is waiting to go on, of person who before was walking.

As who'd had the ear shouted in – by the bicyclist.

Then.

In the car. Over the streets zooming. Where there are passersby everywhere.

———————

Sitting – in the balmy breeze – with the old woman, in chairs, of the alzheimers unit though she is not alzheimers, incarcerated. Sitting with her the two, watch two old men walk, in front of them. Under the sky. The only men around. As the men pass each other ceaselessly, once from no event they shake hands. The one, attractive loose and the manner of what he had been says they won't know what the hell we're doing – but who cares? The hundred-year-old woman sitting seeing this says men aren't as petty as women.

Reading the newspaper in the Middle East – man who'd been against Apartheid in hiding kneeling partly blown by bomb in the street, a few people passersby looking back glancing at him expressionlessly – it is between this, in it – from him having just been blown and torn by the bomb at that minute in the street.

The man shooting solvent on the huge corroded pipe in the heat sweat pouring out of him is the same as the one standing on a deserted beach in Baja with cacti hanging over him naked. A very blue sky behind him who has no clothes on.

The cacti on the desert had begun to bloom. They wandered among the flowers in the intense heat. Then sleeping at night horses came up to them, waking hearing the horses chewing grass close to the couple's ear. The horses shifting, standing next to them.

It being night. Outside. The horses chewing in the dark.

Then sleeping by the ocean at night.

Driving.

There was the sand storm in the day and at dusk in a town.

Miners there in a liquor store, people in the dark then. A warm night.

And then sleeping on the hard metal floor of a ferry with many people curled together and a baby in the dark got up on the young woman's back as she was lying. The baby crawling up on her back in the darkness amidst the bodies.

The ferry crossing the water at night with many people on it.

Dark.

Aqueduct with flat land around it and a moon in the day sky.

At dusk heavy top-lighted clouds animals grazing on the soft green hills.

Dark clouds at night – in order to see them.

Buildings when there are not lights and as that the trees and curving road partly illuminated.

In the darkness, which is what?

The man who was the same one as shooting the solvent onto the corroded pipe standing naked on the desert amidst the cacti and the wide sky by the road, stopped for gasoline. A little boy brings out a gas canister and indicates if the man will sip to have the intake of breath get the gasoline in the spout of the canister to put in the car. Man indicates negative – though gentle tough to little boy kneeling in intense heat of the desert who sips – in breath – of gasoline canister, grimacing if some of it gets in his mouth. Outside. Then.

Curled. Near the man on the hard metal floor of the ferry, who'd stood in the desert – without speaking sleeping among many people on the floor of the boat.

Negative – as that other person – who is him.

Not of the gasoline sipping – but of the man and the child as it happened – him – though their not being related.

Light on the ocean from beach in day light.

Or the light is in it.

That person and that person. Day. That person and that person. Day. Day. That person and that person. Nights. Nights. It's very simple, separate. Day.

The painters returning, in public. Not having been for a long time. One not being in public. That oneself isn't there. Their there. Their not there. The painters not being there. Not being that thing. That one really isn't that. Their being that. Not having been there, in public – or ever to be – and do have that connection. Seeing that.

The connection to society. The painters not having that. Their as valued. Oneself as not. Outside. Their not having it. Their, in public.

Seeing a mature somewhat older man on the street – he's gazing at a crowd of boys, whom he says are going to fight. Say o no they won't or it's not like that. And they erupt socking each other a boy falling head beaten by the others on the sidewalk. On the corner. The crowd of boys running.
   See.

San Francisco.
   Light light sky. Not going back – which that is. Light light. It is back, as being there. Not here, which is San Francisco. Some motion, in this. It's being from this. To there. Which is just in this.

The light of San Francisco. It's wonderful.

In Golden Gate Park. Woman says she'd seen this other woman in her car – had given her, from in the other's car, an opening – at the time of light light.
   It having happened before.

In the Sudan had not occurred – though having been there before. Then. Another time. But occurring a second time, really, in this. It's going to.

Growing up together when they were adults as adults. And a delicate vision, which is open. At the time. Then. Coming to think that's nothing.

A mysterious connection of the painters, painting having returned, to the light. Here.

Though they're in public. Their not there.

Precisely because human society, not in landscapes, had been excluded. Was not here.

There.

Here. But society was not anything.

When you make your move.

Living in front of the entrance ramp to a highway. The cars going up it and others speeding being up on the highway which is held on pillars – hanging gardens.

At dusk and then at night watching the cars.

Watching a car during the day go up the ramp. Races up it. Or a car backs down, slowly. No action, that is before, is like or resembles seeing or the cars going up the ramp or there. It is not a minute motion in this or, before, minute motions in reality.

He says who is a writer he doesn't want to write. Not writing is a good state. He says. Not writing, or wanting to do so, to want to do so – before, as to be a minute motion in reality. Which that is not – when it is in the present.

Dovetailing is that.

Get tough. Being tough. Be tough. Only being that. Getting tough or simply being that. Only being that – so that it's not that. Or and it's not that.

Tough.

His voice makes a sound in his chest – when her ear is to it lying on him. Low melodious.

From in the chest cavity.

That writing or – not writing – would from gearing it changing be able to have life rather than it not be.

To see into life. Which is not in what happens. Is connected to what happens – maybe.

Not here.

Here.

I love paper.

on which things are printed – the loveliness of the paper.

Going in a taxi from the train station – to a place that is to be work, in an (other) city – through blocks of housing that is denuded without window-panes collapsing in which people live – out – in the streets; sitting out, and at the end of that block in the area was the one building that is fixed up and painted. It was the funeral parlor. The funeral parlor.

Man is loaded out on beach with his friends strolling around curve they see a whale which has moldered sheets of skin coming off in which the crabs and birds are.

The carcass rotting of the long grey speckled whale.

And the loaded men strolling.

By the ocean.

The people bathing by the bank with the greenish puffed corpse floating near them and some in a boat grinding their motion picture cameras at the people, they were – afterwards – arrested their cameras taken away from them.

The men, on rocks
of pools and the loaded men went swimming, him unable to tell where the
(cold) water is. Not knowing whether it is at his waist or neck, but that he
cannot breathe water. It is black. The black ripples have colors on them when
moving away from his hands. Swimming in the black. Sleek or slippery, his
skin is that.

My – sitting, in the boat – a man rowing – being rowed, up to along the bank
where the people were bathing. A greenish – blue – corpse, and one of a dog
bloated, with breasts – floated, at the bank.

People were filming, floating near by – weighted, with seven or so in the
rowboat. Being rowed, by or near them.

And the people looking – who're in the water.

Being dumb – as being regarded, and as being something.

Only.

Driving
they had eaten in the small town and then went out in the desert. Feeling ill,
yet driving in the car and then stopping walking out on to the desert. There
was sage, clumps of tangled thorn brush in which the wild horned cattle
stayed. For shade. Going into this to vomit vomiting yet so that the huge cattle flies which tormented them were fierce to the person.

Driving across the country.

For the cattle.

The blonde candidate – empty – dumb, heard on the car radio. So that it
is detached.

It is up – to – death, or in it.

where every one is different

The corpse floating at the bank – decomposing – is not noticed. Not
there.

Earlier, desert river now. No plants except the thorn trees and sage. For
the wild horned cattle.

The vomiting is the inner part of this person, standing in the thorn trees which are where cattle stand out in the heat. Who's just this foolish person as they see themselves

> being dumb – as being something
> only

That's why – the incumbent-candidate – they're standing on the streets.

At night out, a man stood looking into the open door of the restaurant and lit a plastic fork on fire, after lighting his cigarette. Lit the cigarette, and then lit the fork with it.

Then coming in from the open door asks to go to the toilet in the restaurant, to which the very young gracious waiter assents.

There is no thing as a double affirmative which is a negative.

Yeah yeah.

Going up the street.

had

wanted

to have an action – what is that? – it is not a person – it is not anything.

Whales

which have no convention, having been trapped under the ice on their way in the arctic – the ice closed the passage behind them. Their coming up to the still remaining hole for air. The whales being battered.

Ships are there (for the whales) breaking the ice to make a passage for them.

The ships returning to clear huge chunks of ice left in the ships' wake. The floating chunks stopped the whales cutting their snouts and blowholes – they're leaving some blood on the ice.

A whale had disappeared under the sheet of ice – left behind – dead.

A plain, close to the arctic – on which the mosquitoes hatch at the same time as the birds hatch, the species of birds not being able to feed their babies. The chicks simply open their mouths, the masses of mosquitoes filling the plain

Driving the caribou
who flee from the tormenting
which
lose a quart of blood a day from the swarm on the plain – light continually.
in
to the ocean where the herd of caribou stand, up to their necks in the ocean – from them.

———————

Walking toward and by (two) girls, adolescence who have convention one wheeling the other curled in a shopping cart from a Safeway – who were on the corner of Russell and Pine, there was no one around.

So there was no one there.

Blonde adolescent tips the shopping cart being too heavy with the large adolescent curled in it dumping her.

Who remains curled on her side in the cart on its side, crossing the street. In it.

Trees, in the neighborhood.

Walking by, toward them – they're in the middle – of the street, are laughing as squealing giggling cracked up.

That is before they crack up – first laughing when the one adolescent is being wheeled in the shopping cart. Walking by them, behind – they are – dumped from it tipping over in the street, no one around. They were laughing left behind.

———————

The (continually light) plain – mountain range in the background.

though

it is growing night. A humanoid prehensile not far away is standing looking in the direction of the capped ridges – in the plain, naked standing so that the back side of him is visible. The man, half in the light coming from the sky.

Tundra or tough grass is in the foreground.

———————

Bicycling, and at a crossroads in the waste of fields. They are corn fields, evening, some pheasants fly up. Stopping at the crossroads, there's a restaurant which is all-you-can-eat benches with immense obese people eating who're from the farms. Rows of the unrestrained hog-like people – made fragile – sitting, in a crowd.

They scarf, platters of fish brought. More rounds of platters of fish.

The sky outside the restaurant, which is surrounded by the fields, is light evening.

In winter at 20 below zero the restaurants everywhere stands were closed. Playing the video games machine in the one pizza restaurant out in the freezing night. There weren't many people several in it. The glacial arctic camp – outside – with a few people going to it out.

The two people playing the video games

And

coming to the (other) restaurant with the fields surrounding, in the evening in summer – the gluttonous people, from the farms, they were fragile – a din inside. The roads at the crossroad stretching away outside.

The insides of these

The episodes – singly, –

And therefore not meeting anything now, or need for that. Its not meeting anything

in the

Leave the car at some spot bordering the marsh land and walk. On a dirt path, the sky above light light but in swirls – and birds resting or flying. Flocks live there. Walking, airplanes came in to land further on away on the strip but low here. The sky is darkening. She's feeling a little low. Light sky.

Walking alone on the paths of the marsh land which is by the airport the planes coming in, marsh birds living there which are on the water or flying – as it's getting dark not able to find the car walking along the bumper to bumper highway – asking in the dark several business men who come out of an industrial park – their walking from the door – in the black dark who turn away not wanting to speak to a woman who's asking them something. Though one shows the others that her memory of where the car was is verifiable.

She begins walking a long ways.

Her walking in the dark the cars rushing by, the marsh land, birds in the dark – in the car going to the airport lighted from within though not going anywhere meeting someone sitting to it coming in.

On

dirt desert and blue pink or white plastic bags are hanging in twigs on immense plain of dirt immersed in it.

Low plain trees in which are immersed the colored floated plastic trash in the endless dirt, and then sand, plain.

Driving.

Poverty of the straw huts, clump of people in the distance, violently submerged in the endless dust sand which could be the sky that the blue or pink floated bags are immersed in.

Violently as the blue pink or white bags immersed in the low shrub trees, which do not decompose, in the light brown sand as could be the sky.

Coming into a town on the Red Sea. And a single blue bag floats drifting out and in front of the windshields of the trucks and cars at the light.

Dreaming I was not a resident, a passerby, in Italy, at a party where noticing people were in line with trays of food I realized it was a restaurant and stealing I walked out with a piece of meat, raw. I'd crossed the street eating the raw corrugated beef, when a man from the establishment comes out I drop the meat which he didn't see by the sidewalk and asks strongly if I took it. I said no I had left it.

A couple really had driven down a road in the Midwest corn fields the sky hot and still and men drove up alongside sticking their tongues out and shouting fuck you go home. Following them, dragging in the car. Shouting when they are stopped at a stop sign in the midst of the waste of fields.

In the evening there they were sitting at a restaurant out, and young men and women drove by in cars sticking their tongues out, along the street of the town. Up the street slowly or racing, and then back and up it again. Evening, with the fields surrounding the town for miles.

And going in the water, before, when it was the person far out in the day become over-cast floating alone in the inner-tube on the lake. Dark water with only the person on the inner-tube. Which is not cared about.

February 1988

Desert which is immense and from above light brown or red vast rivulets of sand with no human life. As the only land. What land is. Running alongside it and then forward is the deep blue Red Sea – with the edges of the land in very light turquoise blue rim, it is the rim. A very beautiful rim. The people are in the air. There are patches of sand in, as it goes on, the endless sea, the very light turquoise rimmed. So it could be sky, which has white rainless clouds. In the sky or it could be in the sea.

Whatever is darker as shadows could be just in the air. Only in the air. Sand patches, rimmed or with the very light blue shallower sea. But only if one's here.

Going on road to dusty town. Huge clouds hanging low in dusk. Brown or white clusters or walled of town – with a blue door. Only blue doors. Women in black heavily veiled but at a distance or on side road. In red sky from it being dusk but to one side of it being dusk. Small airplane – is – placed – on the roof of a low building. Call to prayers so a voice is through the town.

Continual call to prayers or praying of many voices – singing. Supreme depression. Silence.

Supreme depression of it not being land – though it is land.

The white flecks that may be only in the air. Or may be in the Red Sea. Later lying, in one's body which had been depressed.

Black night – warm. But didn't go out.

In the desert, driving in the morning – waves of light brown sand with the small green bushes. Which is not the sky, just desert. Then. Sand on the road, washing over it – is in the sky, is it.

Lighted from the street light. Which is the night.

Streets of the town in the night or day are brown with dust – from the desert. Where the storks flew in the trees but that was to one side, in the streets at night crowds strolling in the dust – in George's hotel congregation of relief workers of the famine, coming here from it, their children there, sitting, encamped in his hotel – and in the street at night hollow feeling of only boys begging in the brown dust of the center of the town.

Sitting drinking an orange soda on a terrace of an old hotel in front of the Nile where people come men in the long white robes – this is at the time of their war, famine in one part – storks fly, having a nest, in the leafy tree among them, in and out and out on the Nile and in V's above the people in the dusk blue sky which is then dark, the row of trees is lit from beneath from the lights. Dark blue above and then black night and in this the feeling that the surface of what the people here are doing is not that.

The back and neck strained and hurt she rolls gently from the bed to her knees and feet to rise. It is morning. The storks flying among the trees is another day. Their bellies against the light blue sky. People passing. Bathing or fishing in the Nile by lorries people, dust but sometimes by it where there are only a few people the night and day are in time the same but separate from the intense heat.

Driving around to different parts of the town, there is a sand storm. Brown sky. The morning, in which she had slid from the bed to her knees to rise. Very gentle manner of people. In a taxi, to leave. The doors of the airport are locked, with a crowd outside, from the sand storm. The planes may not fly, very gentle won't answer, may be. Going away from the airport, coming back. The doors are opened – above is brown with the sand. In the air.

Solitude.

The packed train going over the desert – jammed people – avarice of drivers before in towns and passersby – sitting in the train car at the beginning the body goes into a shut-down decline holding-still, no eating or pissing or feeling with the body though conscious – in the dash to the ocean which is at the far end of the land – and after the train driving, the driver having to stop and pray – a boy selling Pepsi by the road leads graciously to the urinal of the Mosque.

Leads past angry set faces – to the urinal – the kindness of the boy.

Squatting and pissing – out of the body that is still holding-still.

This will be reaching this. So that it does not meet anything. Only with the minute movements of the other people – masses of people.

Wind – in light wind – blowing through – out on highway in shining blue and pale sand with trucks blowing by in shimmer waver of heat – stopping three times with flat tires with now no spares, two taxi young men working bent one hitchhiking away with the tires – trucks baa-baaaa blast of horn going by – going by sideways so the highway isn't seen and dark blue truck is in the light blue sky – or forward with light wind coming through.

notes on:

The Night

To not do rhetoric – so that it is jammed in on itself – and there is no rhetoric. And is the inside of this.

The word

night

Back. Though it is recent.

Boys in the dusty town – come up lightly gently to beg. There's a famine in the desert country – and a war – the men in the dust-filled street seeing the boys come lighting up to ask the others lash at them to disperse them.

Entering on foot the dusty streets hollow in the center of the town. They've been left by the taxi. Going into a dive hotel, the man who's carrying their bags lashing aside at a young boy coming up – into a hotel with many street entrances. The lattices and doors are broken from entries in the town.

To have a conversation – not the way it is spoken, but the way it is heard.

Listening rather than, or more so than, speaking. People.

And masses of people.

To see the town – sand blowing, the driver of the taxi gentle soft spoken and out by the Nile boy bathing, his donkey is in the Nile – only listening, few people, as between that – where the storks flying in the trees are to one side just there, not in the hollow center of the town.

No sound – is that.

Having been there before.

In the same hotel, as a child – that is there – though as it happens it is not the dive that is in the hollow center of the town, or George's. Is no sound. Not the sound in doing this. The burned—out—intense dusty town had been then also.

loving it.

Come into the crowded, stoops, August, city. On the subway—boys, women, in any combination of clothes since it's this

People in anything—or no shirts.

Their

Strolling, they smell the sewers from the hot city. There are few people. The taxi coming in—to the serene city at night through the streets.

The taxi going—just it.

Where the gutted neighborhoods had been—and are.

And not them—for through the streets.

It's empty.

People on subway, which comes out into clear open day on its way to Coney Island. And get there, no one there—but a few toddlers in puffed inflated suits for it's winter being strolled on the boardwalk in the wind.

The train.

People calling in the warm night, which comes up to the apartment window.

Up to the redlights—in the evening the taxi going up to them through the streets in August.

Though they have Sharia—pictures in the newspaper of boys in a group posed who have their hands and a leg amputated for they had been stealing.

Listening.

That is the move.

Is.

That one—why is that?

incredibly aged in her nineties woman who's the landlady is seen in the distance ahead out—dragging cart far from her home, by the Safeway. Is island serene

place

and is being
put
into a cop car by the cop who's seen her out

not knowing her

and is going to give her a lift

He's tucking her in – seen from far back.

San Francisco.

at night – yet in the empty (serene) center where there is the city hall and the opera house and a park. In front of the city hall, many many people lying covered by blankets. Rows in the moonlight and slight streetlight of covered outlines who sleep.

The police cars here and there roam in the street. Around – casually. Not having anything to do with them.

They're not bothering them.

My – walking through the park of the rows of lined up people lying on the ground with a blanket over them.

The moon slightly obscured above them (the) (others).

The taxi dashing up of empty night serene area – of clogged millions street. Who also lie in a row on the sidewalks where they sleep. Each is on their back. A cover is stretched up from their feet over their face.

honking empty – the taxi

by row of people covered.

People taking a nap on the ground in the railroad station with the crowd rushing by – in the crowd – who pull the cover held by their feet over their face.

Woman lays down her babies in a line – in the open warm night – with the crowd going by.

These people who're not seen – covered – under the sky in the park at night

When I was leaving a reading – walking through the park.

A man kicked me – not here – (some other time) on 5th Avenue with a crowd streaming along. It was because I was angry – to myself, walking. He was a crazy – he kicked me so hard

He lived out there.

And I stood, not moving – as he screamed at me, people smirking pouring by – I was going to leap on him and beat him, until an old white-haired man drew me along – Come on.

Hearing, that they came in with guns to the other hotel, George's there where the relief workers sitting in the room and shot and shot killing seven there—for the same time—there only, if one isn't there—which I wasn't, and these people here aren't there—and their there.

So that their and one's mind is free.

They would have had to go up the stairs, past the office—with the open doors.

They apprehended a man who'd just stepped down to the corner still with the machine-gun in his hand—men nearby the hotel wrestling out of white robes, having just blown away the people in the hotel.

The next day and which is not vacant.

Coming into a city. Late at night

Going in the taxi—(it had occurred before)—at night, warm, and coming to where an other cab on the sidewalk had been left—cracked up with a bus that's left, beside it, on the walk—in the moonlight—the driver of the taxi that's going by it—hearing—the drivers on the taxi radio comment on the taxi there.

Not doing that—since it was before.

No one is around.

Their speaking to each other.

the one going up to it which is on the street,

through the streets—that it will may be stripped (they conjecture)—there.

Though the taxi going by it up through the streets. And cracked up—which is in that. Or—the taxi may or it may not be stripped, at night, out, warm. Which is a city—though serene—so it is the reverse.

The city which is the reverse of it. Them and the taxi going up by it. Leaning out in the moonlight to see the other cab.

Going in this country into—in the middle of it—the small blue VW, as if moving ahead through the sea of grass which is on either side of the road—having a canoe on it—so that the boat goes into the tall waves of grass—beginning in the middle of the country.

The canoe on it.

As a rudder. It overlaps the small blue VW—tied on it.

The car goes past fields of grass—on and on, parted on the sides.

Tall corn.

There are grain bins—and the bending tall grass on either side of the road.

Farmers, who haven't farmed for many years – paid not to, surplus, so that they ride into the restaurants in their big cars – in the towns – and have no connection – cannot drop off body and mind – to anything – and now they're poor, and haven't even gardens.

The farmers having to be paid from their lovely cattle being branded on the foreheads by the government to be destroyed. As surplus. The cattle are being branded – are standing – out. The angels heavily hanging fluttering in the air.

There was a dark sky with swirls – a couple bicycling through or by the corn fields, a dog chasing them, with the tornado siren going.

The angels fluttering in a flock – but heavily – in the one area.

So that they – angels – are not with the cattle, or having anything to do with them.

The light of the sky on the green meadow.

It is the reverse of here.

The later car with the canoe on it – to – the other cab, cracked up in the moonlight – but which is not in the middle.

This is in the middle of the country.

The man asked – would you take your Austrian mother there, in (some) (other) old car, and the man from the filling station said yes but would buy her a bus ticket from there. So they went to the desert in it – where there was only a filling station out in the desert. Locking the keys in the trunk and the man at the filling station went in coming out shot the lock of the trunk off it.

It is a low wrecked Buick.

The later one

on the two-lane road

the car with the canoe on it – which overlaps it – tied on it.

And (some) (other) man – traveling – his clothes, which he'd locked in his jammed car's trunk, it's cold – no heat in the car – with a blanket wrapped on him, wearing a tee-shirt with numbers written on the front, goes into a hotel. So they (others) say your kind is not here. They stay somewhere else – to – the run-down hotel down the street. Where he stays there.

In Salt Lake City. Where there are the bums in the Greyhound Bus station.

He was going across the country.

Some other time not the one of the car with the canoe – tied on it.

I ran into the lobby of a dingy hotel – from the car – and young women were screaming at an older woman about their keys. She at them. They all screamed at once invective. Silence as one. I asked the cost of a room for a night. They all looked at me sympathetically, meaning you don't want to come back as I went back out to the waiting car

And went to some (other) place that smelling of urine. A sheet on the bed and no towels. Going down to the lobby again to ask for these, the clerk calls the maid Fred, it's a couple. Doors closing and opening. All night.

Driving

from the city – at night – fireflies came right up to the car. lit flits. Along side the car. The night was that warm.

The canoe, of the car.

Tied on it. Not that time.

Girls in the subway are on cocaine they say screaming to each other – as if to start a fight with (others) around them – they're derogatory about their own color, as if that were funny though not really – and real.

The people in the subway look down – it's night, late, alone of the girls screaming to one another. We are without hope.

A man was seated nearby them, kissing a woman. Turning from smooching her, he took out a can of hair spray, spraying his head again and again. The girls stopped screaming noticing him. He said distortedly come over here sweetie

to them.

In the same, the next day. Traveling. My – lost – out – in front of a train station. Misery, tired, the tears coming. A poor man came up to me on the street indicating to an (other) building

Did you know that they built this building – (which cast a shadow) – so that I couldn't sit in the sun?

Do you believe that – ?

I don't know. He said:

> So great is the hatred of people, that they
> put it there so that we couldn't sit down

No one would stop for me. When I'd stepped out in the street, the passersby sneered

(I turned away down the street, trying to catch cabs – which wouldn't stop. Stopped one – standing in the middle.)

(We're) – as going

Others, low wrecked Buicks or the Cadillacs men in the streets in the town which is vacant, blocks, neighborhoods, stores – there is not gutted, as it is always vacant. Without it being gutted or vacant

Either.

to what. The men out, on the street who're unemployed – it is not that. And corner

stores

or in the middle of the block. A man crossing to another or standing in small groups.

Out.

And

others, people coming out of the entrance to the Golden Gate race track – seeing them, when going by on the freeway. A crowd pouring out. That is by the town of the men who're out, just them – or one of them crossing to others – in the street. And it not being a city or vacant.

Yet people are in the city

They won't know what they're doing – or caring.

Their in the city. And no constructions of the city, and is that. Is those constructions of the city.

It isn't that – and who cares?

Is not the light city.

———————   ———————   ———————

A couple – terrain where the young men and women had leaned out of the cars sticking their tongues out driving the length of the town, in the evenings, the fields surrounding the town for miles – Got into the canoe, going down the river.

Muskrats are seen along the bank – the two people holding oars in the canoe, going downstream.

murmurs of the extremely elderly people – floor of them out – turning in their wheelchairs – moaning or sighing – floor of them – weeping as one passes, not speaking – up the hall – the turning, of their wheelchairs simply of that.

There's a bluff of the canoe, the streams finger out, – confluence – on a plateau – and the sole canoe drifts out onto it.

Seeing a building sometime in the vegetation, they draw up to the shore. Not struggling. Out there it is a Frank Lloyd Wright building squat as if sliding into the river, and inside it young women in green velvet floorlength gowns as of a pooltable, and one in white floorlength playing a harp as tasteless food is served – the people having come from the canoe finding it.

In the vegetation.

Then the bluff from the canoe, and looking over it – the streams finger out – onto the plateau.

The sole canoe.

Appendix to *The Return of Painting*. The following is simply vision. It is not part of the novel. (since there is not a novel.)

The comic book

She sat on a small red sofa, up stairs in a café crowded with people. The room had been empty when she'd come in. It filled so that the chairs were taken. A man sits down beside her on the red seat. A woman who's part of this group, standing over her looking down on her wanted her to rise. Saying to give her her seat.

Mt. Lassen with the clear, still lake in front of it, and the fur trees. I love pictures. To touch the pretty pictures. Light in the center. The light brown boulders preceding the lake – which look out over it.

She's a sort of tight sweater version of Lana Turner unconscious spoiled. Brutal making scenes. A little high school girl, in her thirties, smoldering who could cry and be hurt. She looks down waiting for the other to submissively yield her seat. Cigarette clouds in the air. People talking, in the bar. The other sat, without moving or speaking until Lana Turner walks away.

The (other) woman goes downstairs and out of the bar – and down the street at night. Her heels ring on the pavement of the empty block.

There're a crowd of men with packs crouched in the dark door of a closed restaurant. They're what used to be called hobos – coming into town, with packs – sitting on the sidewalk – there's always many of them. Here there's a mood of night hostility. As if it might be ugly. She's walking near them – across the street, with her heels – one called to her asking for money. Turning her head to him simply it's as if it is carried by a wind her body whirling and dashed on the sidewalk on her hip with terrible force.

Quiet hushed of the men in the squatting group. They are sympathetic.

From across the street in the dim doorway.

She fell with force as if the body were a bruise. Soft. Flesh encasing the hip – the bone, only that. And got up with great pain hurt very badly limping, going down the block passes the lighted windows of the stores.

The comic book is the self.

She'd seen her before. In a restaurant café at a distance a skirmish arises where Lana a poor man has come in from the street perhaps is going to ask for something but you don't know begins screaming at him.

Lana humiliates him. In the restaurant, he's just someone beats a retreat.

The crowd goes on talking or resumes talking in the restaurant.

The waves off the cliffs in the center but really the deep thick billows of the grey ocean the body of water itself – the swells.

It was a warm night in San Francisco so that never happens and there's a dance near the opera house and by the city hall serene city center. One of the dancers the girl comes out to the edge of the stage pressed up to the audience with hardly any clothes on. The dance has a thought.

The plumes of the yucca plants many of them standing here and there in the field in the desert behind the pale sky.

So then she is introduced to the man – the group is in trucking, and have a sense of only money mattering the conjunction of a tenuous line of that.

There are no friends.

That's the constellation. A system which is continuous because it is empty.

The other people from the audience do not seem to be like them – are jovial, in a good mood. In a swirl around them, at the table with the long sheet of salmon.

A dead man is in the subway. He's lying on the ground, the trains coming in and out – face up, waxen – bluish – blondish dirty mat of hair. The people step around him.

He already seems to be rigid –

One thing is only a mode of another.

At some other time in a restaurant. Seated in a crowd across the table from a steely-blue-eyed man in the group in trucking, though not the man who was in charge met in the vestibule.

The man who'd been in the vestibule, seeming mean – on top of her – putting his long stem into her.

Her coming. Or he does first

and the somewhat mean demeanor of his is not insurmountable –

They are together.

her, when out, repeating what he says – who's in trucking – and repeating it very determinedly. That is what there is, the conjunction.

He puts his long stem into her – her bucking. So that he comes from being on top of her.

Her coming when he hadn't yet.

The development of the port. A row of ships are docked – she walks along on the dock, gangplanks, checking for the name of the ship.

There'd been a funeral and going to it carrying the ashes with them, in the rain for many hours all along the way cars wrecked or stopped left along the turnpike on the way passing the city which is in the distance people in rest-stops crowded in the sheets of rain and they get to the green grass. In the cemetery.

The steely-blue-eyed man is there. Near-by, on the dock. The huge wooden crates are lifted and swing from the deck of the freighter. Deposited.

It is only here. Singly. Having come through the blue bay and into Oakland the developing port.

The (other) woman pulls out in her car. From the entrance to the docks. Cranes are against the sky.

> ocean – water lapping
> around
> a dock – on which were tracks
> from a railway line with
> water in them

She goes down a road, men riding caterpillars reared above the buildings. She's walking. Some time goes by. Around the bend, trucks come with men who're workers bobbing in them. They look at her casting eyes down sideways as if contemplating as they go by.

Raining, she holes up in her apartment her hip and leg hurting.

The place is a tiny matchbox. It has been invaded by ants, though there is no food in it. The ants infested a plant. Streams of them, making a nest in it. They come, searching, running across the bedcover – in which she is in the bed – and she reaches out and kills some, another row coming. The infested plant died which she replaced with a glass of water with flowers. The ants appeared suddenly rushing in streams up the side of the glass.

One of the men living outside sleeping at night probably in the rear of the Safeway or a strip of vegetation behind a building. He doesn't speak ever dressed in rags that'd become so filthy people'll give him something else. Then he wears that.

People speaking to him, when he's out, in the same area. Matted, dirty, no shoes never speaks. And once he's on the telephone, the pay phone out on that same corner where he is, speaking into it fast smiling. Never seen him smile.

He'd been sleeping in people's vans – and a neighbor woman says he'd stolen cats to eat them and she puts up signs on telephone poles around to that effect.

He slept on the floors in other people's vans.

The group in trucking – the freighter having left from the port at midnight and sailed. So now there's no way to get on it. Getting up the gangplank getting past it on it, hadn't happened.

The (other) woman goes to see the steely-blue-eyed man, lean muscular body seated in his trucking line office. He speaks in a curt way.

His stem having been in a blinking young woman stumbling her speech not drunk or is so. Holding her cigarette, sitting across at the table in the restaurant. And blowing the smoke thinly through her nostrils.

To put his stem into her.

Him on her – with the stem in her. The (other) woman trembles under his gaze which does not make connection, or did not attempt to attract. The stem pulled out, and put in again.

He puts it in to her again.

The billowing ocean open sea freighters, froth on that freighter that's out already.

Going out to a restaurant, simple clatter in it. And sees at a distance Lana Turner who's rude to the waiter, shouting – from afar, the crowd talking.

The steely-grey-eyed man – blue. His hard muscular legs. He's unconscious, curtly. His stem is out.

To have the stem in her.

This is open.

The steely-blue-eyed man had been talking to the matted ragged fellow who lives out sleeping in people's vans, the time he'd been on the telephone smiling. Defenseless.

Eyes up – face blank – empty, dead in the yard, where the wreck cars are on the street. Trash in strayed shopping carts, the genre which is just (this), on the street. It had rained. A porch up to a depleted paint peeling house, the sky light from it, and the matted fellow stiff lump lying in the wet yard.

———

Not drugs – or it may be, the fellow in rags – free is free. It is not easy. Empty. Floating or not floating, living outside. One wants to live in cars – other than him. Doing so for an – time, not that.

The (other) woman had been married to someone who then lived in cars afterwards. From year to year. Living out of the car, and free.

And in this there are the drugged – not them.

Highway 5 is a strip for many many miles of waste. It is the interior of no man's land waste with strips of truck tires strewn. And in the center on the way there is a corral, herds of many hundreds of cattle. The cattle stand in the corral herded in the midst of the waste, and an establishment like a spa hotel sprawling dining empty room composed of rawhide and to serve the meat.

> The entire place
> The cars drifting past fast

She drove to L.A. seeing the old woman the mother of the ragged man of the vans – who coming to the door looks past her as if the (other) woman weren't there. Immediately the dazed wants to be taken on errands as if she'd come for that, driven to the bank pausing while she goes in. To have her lawn mowed, which is done sweating mowing it in the humid L.A. day near boulevards.

Man out on empty boulevard snarling at dog get down get over here.

The dazed screeches, an exclamation or a wild cry and the Chrysler stopping, she strolled on the other's arm a few feet to the display window of a shoe shop looking in lovingly. Having collected the items wrapped in tissue dozens of shoes which she didn't wear and smart suits since she was before in business.

> and relax – so
> that it
> just opens – and
> completely
> relaxes

The cop with cigar in mouth legs planted apart sat in his office with his weight pushed forward – his stem out – and is the same as this (this). Light – fragile. Wanting. The muscular fat in his cheeks worked. To be interpreting – first – ahead of it in order to have it.

It is defined as that.

In the barn the warehouse with the television cameras taking as of the cattle – drifting – of the evangelical ministry the people jumping and swooning for Christ under the effect of the minister speaking to the grinding – boulevards of L.A., on them in the Chrysler. They stand up here and there jumping to their feet in the auditorium. Beside the (other) woman the little dazed bat is blissfully standing in the third row.

Girl standing by filling station in overalls.

Driving on the boulevards in the Chrysler – lets out screeches in the car.

The dead body of the little bat – is on the floor, in the kitchen. She'd fallen on morphine – though it is not that – some on drugs – in her thin slip succumbing to the cold without the heat on, in the clement L.A. Where the temperature had fallen briefly. The little lump lying there.

At the grave site, the evangelical minister jumping – jumping-jack – clicking his heels in the air glad that she is dead.

The hearse pulled away over the cemetery knolls.

The ragged man who'd slept in the vans is Lana's brother.

She seems to be outside fixing her lawn with something like hairspray.

The Chrysler in the drive. Mowing the lawn for her the sweat on the person springing out on their back.

The cop with the cigar in his mouth seated pushed forward is the same, internal – as the insides of these episodes – singly, empty – such as the little bat's death. The small lump found lying crumpled in hypothermia on the kitchen floor.

In Silver Springs.

Driving from there.

The line of snowy peaks ranges running from west to east. Balancing this is a still, limpid lake in the center surrounded by purple ranges. The lake. Singly, the line of peaks range running from north to south. And so it's free.

The steely-blue-eyed man is seen in the town – the dick looking at him.

The view (this)

The lights a string of lights of the town on the desert. That are in day faded. Inside the cardboard facade is a pool in which is Cleopatra's barge floating with her gold petalled.

The (other) woman sits across from the boss at a little table of the casino – searching for a job in Las Vegas – who sat weight pushed forward, lids heavy jowled, delicate, and said she would have to wear risqué hesitating in the midst of the word outfits.

The cattle herds aren't here, though some stand here and there in the desert. Weed. The trucks coming in from the desert – and their who live there gambling in the town. Which is lit up with beads covering the buildings at night.

In the day it is pale pink and sky.

The little flat houses, in one of which I lived.

To the edge of the town.

Sky there, weeds – a nude man standing on the plain of the desert floor.

She is involved with a shill whom she sees standing in his suit working by standing pretending to play at the roulette tables.

His stem out – at night.

Though he works at night. Afterwards.

Someone else – saying – their distorting reality does so at the risk of someone wanting what's real. Which is, in that sense. The trucks coming in from the desert

And she works serving. A waitress. And the honest delicate man boss is blown in his car smattered in the parking lot of the casino. Blam the fiery folding like a flower. He'd reported his earnings honestly to the IRS. Larger casinos said they had less. There were no drugs. It is easy.

It was easy to kill him. Or not to.

Drifting fast across L.A. on high freeways in the Chrysler, she'd suddenly had her arm gripped and pinched gouged with nails by the little blissful bat. The cracked bat, there was no occasion for this, stared meanly into her eyes as she hurt her. The mean empty thing. She wanted her to know she was purposely hurting her. Who was this?

Not weeping – because that would please the little bat.

The spattered man who'd leaned forward seated heavy lidded delicate. Seated in the then empty casino. A business man – of that above ground.

She gets to the house of the steely-blue-eyed man on the outskirts of town. Flat houses. A screen door, which she opens – he is dead in the house. Wood statuary flat boats with figures holding oars rowing hang in such movement it is as if they were flying sailing.

The flat long boats with the rowers span the entire length of the room.

They jut along forward. As if the oars were dipping. The man is lying as if sleeping with his throat cut. His eyes are open, blue but they are losing the color.

He had had nothing to do with the delicate heavy-lidded heavy boss being blown and scattered in his car. That seems reasonable.

It is reasonable.

Mesas with the pink light filtering down the corrugated butts – and the fir trees standing – not here.

As could the mesquite desert which is right up to the edge of his house compare, singly, to the hills of San Francisco – he wasn't from either – either

The desert with cacti stretching wildly – solitary – around the border, with the low long cars which has beads a Jesus figure hanging on the dash. Racing forward in it – not the throat cut

Free, as it's there

He is

Lana is intelligent but in an inchoate manner. Unconscious warm. Mean. Not dumb, but under her husband's control. He says of people that they are small out to gain. (He loves her.) Yet she could have been desperate.

Oakland is fragile, the dawn coming up, the shopping carts standing along the deserted neighborhood street trash brimming out of it which people picked on, the wreck cars there.

Mostly trash on the block here and there, in the morning, driving coming through the neighborhood to the soft port.

By the place where the ragged fellow had been found a lump lying in the back yard.

Through the mesquite desert – though – the low long car with the beads hanging driving. The person getting out, the car beached, and slitting the throats of the lizards which had been collected and carried in cages in it because they had died. In the heat of the desert. He had slit their throats and strung them up to get the blood saving at least that, they had already been dead. Out there in the waste.

Some federales come along in their car. It is easy. They stop seeing him, out there.

They approach him, yet see what he is doing. Get back in the car, and drive away hurriedly. In the baking desert.

> having to screw that up
> on it so it's
> screwed around

He the blue-eyed man goes on through a town that has a factory. Cotton strands presumedly from it are washing along the sides of the road and fill the air floating in it. There is a wind through. Poor men are by the road.

Of Oakland – soft, empty. The filling stations and a department store.

The other woman goes down in the port. Opening the garage door of a large domed garage. Pans of oil are stretched on the floor of the garage. Lana is dead lying a lump as the poor ragged man on the floor, amidst the pans of car oil.

In the pans are gardenias floating with the perfume – the scuz the film of oil on the garage floor streaked.

The gardenias float a few on the surface of the thick oil – in the pans which are here and there throughout the warehouse-like floor.

The pans are set out here and there. Her lying among them.

The President says meanly sneering that his ancestors had come over on the Mayflower – weren't immigrants. Meaning that he was white – and the public elected him. An action. There are no actions.

Gardenias are in the oil of the pans around her.

There'd been a funeral, and having gone to it in the line viewing the corpse and the mourners having to take the hand and speak to the widow their coming down from the corpse, who's sitting facing the platform. Waxen stiff. The line becomes an ordeal for her since she's weeping – she's Chinese, most of the mourners were. Looking into her eyes, so that the shock is too much for her, too intimate. She is an older very lovely woman, who is shaking like a flower forward racked shaking tremors out.

Wanting to stowaway, and so having checked the newspapers for the departure time and destination of the freighter. And with fear getting on it sneaking up the gangplank, when watching, to the deck. It leaves at midnight. The chugging of the engine in the center of the freighter. It goes out across the sheet of bay. The freighter engine churning passes slowly under the bridge.

The grey billows swells mass of the ocean.

In the middle.

Grey blankets swells of the ocean's bulk.

Hiding in a cardboard box – but having nothing to eat, and so after three days she's driven out from hiding by hunger and is caught.

Having been driving in the area where the ragged man had been lying – wrecks – and see two men pushing shopping carts with trash in them in the block where there are always shopping carts heaped with the trash – o Oakland, soft.

Women go by, standing – the car goes by – on the corner where they're always out standing. In a silver mini-skirt, and boots.

It's hot, a wind blowing so that pigeons blow through the air.

Yet the grey blankets swells of the ocean's bulk.

Or simply that of mass of humped ocean grey swells

73

The players running around on the turf in the background, kicking the ball – under the night lamp – calls come up from them. The unnaturally bright green of the turf from the lamps.

But the green of the turf emanates from the thin lightened night – Lana Turner has concern for her brother the ragged man without speaking sleeping out wet in the yard.

Getting down into it. Her swimming like an otter. From the freighter, weak on a heavy mass ocean and then out on a plateau terrace of rows of blue waves that were rough, dragging in them, the heavy dark clouds overhead. To the sand.

She was walking in the surging rough water. comes in to the sand. A couple were lying sleeping on the beach, not moving for a long time – a while. And then the man's knees ham coming up

The players throw up the ball, from their feet, running – on the filtered lightened green. Lana, who has nothing – to do – with them, is standing with the man who'd been met in the vestibule who's in charge, her husband.

There is nothing but the air, forward, now. That is always true.

The ragged man had been lying a lump dead in the yard. The man of the vestibule loves Lana – thinking that people are small and out to gain.

They're partly lightened by the lamp.

She's standing out angry dark lunging.

The

steely-blue-eyed man with his throat cut and lying backward, the neck released – it is easy to live freely – in the room with the wooden, long flat boats flying; that is not from the man who's in charge who was in the vestibule.

The blue-eyed his chest slender the hard muscle of his legs – who'd put his stem in the stammering woman – afterwards – in the long low, desperate anxious, car beads and the Christ figure hanging on the dash swinging, goes in the desert.

He's weeping.

There. The wild cattle, which are long-horn, walk in a line. Thorny sparse shrub – the cattle stand here and there – is in front of them.

Lana is already dead streaked by the oil in the garage. Lunging, angry. And the blue-eyed man.

He feels ill. Getting to a hotel, he barely communicates for it and makes it up the stairs to his room. He falls on the bed. Feels a terrible sense of illness. Outside at night, the trucks careen the drivers shouting; and he lies on the bed. For the night. Then there's a moment of quiet; his muscles relax lying on the bed. The cocks begin crowing everywhere, keeping him disturbed.

Anyone can do this. if it has ability and that other if it does not have ability are doing the same thing. And doing it in the same way. Has no other function.

This is in it, the same.

The cop heavy leaning forward the cigar in his mouth – imposing the delicate doctrine which doesn't explain anything, before. Putting it there before, and he may be – is the same.

to be free.

Though he has the plodding delicate obtuse doctrine that is not outside. And is tough and brutal in crushing his opponent. Bears down, with a mind like gravel. Slow. Has beat up some of the men.

in the port

She wavers. Meeting with a man who's a sort of jock, out by the garbage cans.

She'd seen him running trotting up and down the street. Then in to his apartment, the lights go on. The lawn in front. And out by the garbage cans – he is in misery, had wanted only to be what his father is. Had wanted to be just conventional. He didn't have a job. He was alone.

It's dusk.

Man had stuffed the dog barking into the window of the people who owned it on their table when they were eating.

The dog had been barking right in front of them, in front of the open window.

She responding to him saying what he wanted by the garbage can turning say Well at least you were spared that – meaning being only conventional.

He smiles a sickening smile.

to her.

Trotting in front of the apartment house – in the street back and forth loping covering a long distance.

Evening and she is in a café. That shines out on the freeway overpasses up, little tables are in it. The rich salesman of the sort of used cars, sipping his wine – sits at the table with her. She is speaking to him.

He's yellow, clean through. And shows it openly.

He does not know desperation – the loping hyena who'd been trotting up and down the block. Who'd thought he was ill, had no job, or really respectability – convention – opulence

The people in the café are there sitting looking. so they are the same as him. But he is yellow.

The sort of used car salesman is not in trucking. He values money. He's greedy. Sitting at the table. it is one to one – Associated with them. Though he is mean, machine minute – in which people are mere functions.

Though they are sitting looking, in the café.

She feels completely desperate.

The steely-blue-eyed man running ill in the hotel below the border, lying on the bed the trucks blaring at night. Sweating feeling ill. Weeping then.

He'd the blue-eyed man'd killed the ragged man.

Lump drifting wet in the yard.

He's talking. The man feeding in cafés is oddly stagnant. A fly on the gazelle.

They are the same as him, in the café. Though he is a fly on the gazelle. They aren't.

It seems.

She gets up. The freeway overpasses go on lightened in the dim light of the evening outside, packed with the crush of cars.

She has a sense of that being what this is. She is in the gourmet section of the town.

She then sees the man who'd been met in the vestibule, who's in charge. He is on the dock. It is after–Lana is dead. A cargo is being lifted to the wharf. In it was a corpse.

It is there.

Cops are all over the wharf. The murdered man is a driver for him. He from the vestibule is contemplative to her–though.

Meaning softly Don't be angry. No voice. The long low cars with the beads and the Christ figure on the dash swinging–coming into L.A.

A man lying in the street from automatic rifle fire. Another man with a red stain on his chest lying there. These figures dying alone out, in public. Only– the man from the vestibule is one of these poor.

At her funeral, the evangelical minister–jumping, jumping-jack–the man from the vestibule saying Get back, to him.

Passing through the halls and the old people are out softly moaning or weeping in the ward. Without words, looking off. Sitting. Turning in their wheelchairs not at her as she goes through.

Get me out of here. A woman lies with her mouth open, emaciated. Un-moved. Another in the bed next to her weeping saying that.

The emaciated hollowed out woman lies on one leg–the other leg, with its foot on the bed–her mouth open, through this not hearing apparently. Get me out of here, the other says.

She gets out onto the hot freeway

from here

Do you suppose that we will all end this way yes

Innumerable filling stations and stands on it. Above the wrinkled rivulets of the mountains below seem to be smoldering as purple hotbeds.

The trotting man–touring up and down the street in the evening. Dragging a dog up the stairs – that had been barking – and the woman comes out lunging.

In the midst of the country – in the grass lands and fields – and yet there are only porno, with just the one theater in a town – separated out there.

The lighted beaded freighter seen forward. So that it comes forward – docked – in the soft Oakland port. And then on it, having snuck on getting into a cardboard box, and out on the open sea.

Pink corrugated roof of clouds in the evening.

The (other) woman goes up onto the porch of his apartment, taking the back steps. The door is swinging, tapping in the wind. In the Berkeley night. He is alive. Sitting. Smiling his sickening smile. There is no bluff – or is. (Him trotting on the street, with the sweat dropping off him in dashes – in the evening)

The cop heavy delicate says it's gangs. Car folds burning like a flower. The man from the vestibule who says people are small out to gain – yet he's there. Defenseless. The low cars beads and the Jesus figure swinging from the dash – the same, with him – its gears, tires screeching isn't folded in the poor

Why are you doing this? It is that for everyone. There are gaps. Though they may occur over years. And they are innocent

were anyway

Driving in the balmy humid night on the greenish overpasses with the city lit before. Vegetation – it is easy to live freely. From the freighter.

Mountain ranges and the ocean on them from on the ground, and that being, is putting it back through itself in that sense.

A woman giving out three orgasmic moans and the screens closing all along the balcony.

Going swimming the man who'd
had to go

<pre>   digging in caves in the army in the war when
                 he'd been
                 ordered not to swim
</pre>

A black mounted truck cab with the huge tires coming across on the red roads of the fields. Crossing the fields, red dirt wake. This. A man stepping down, shooting the manager tough sensitive who'd been there – and is running. Begins running – on – being – hurt. And in the field.

Cattle their reddish and white kneeling as if in a nest floating in an area of brown dry grass. The man gets in lying with them.

The man who'd been met in the vestibule in charge, the hump of his back bending over the dead streaked white rag in the domed vaulted garage around them.

There is not a noise around them.

Of this. Yet to come out with this. This is such fragile and meagre engrained matter as to be indistinguishable.

It is that.

T's dream.

<pre>   his hair's slicked back as in the 40's
                 but in it I and he are aware it
                 and he resembles his father
</pre>

(who died, recently)

<pre>   and seeing him younger having
                 a sexual being, or movement
                 that he didn't know of him
</pre>

Plantation fields stretching away, with roads through them. Isolated, no one.

This is lava bed at the base with the ocean on it – as if it were molten, sometimes fiery flow going into the waves.

Not saying anything.

Climbing the hill, in the light of evening the clouds hovering, a reddish and white calf was kneeling lying in a hole in the side of the hill. There is a raw wound on the calf's back on which the flies lit. Misery.

In it. The center of it.

A field of birds is on the ground singing to each other.

A man says of someone that she'd say she was depressed out and get on a plane and come off wearing – something – emerald rings. Same of him

>   says says in
>   humans

Bright day for miles across the bay and out onto the overpass – a cabby, driving, keeps balking wanting to go back – can't go so far – though he knows a sign out and is comforted at knowing where he can drop her.

She goes, walking, to the apartments where the man had trotted in the street, before.

In back, in the rear, a thin older wisp of a woman comes to the porch, up stairs. She is drunken and a plate has been put in her mouth of teeth a thin rim of blood on the rim of her gum.

The drunken thin woman speaks in a husky manner still with a dignity and a rim wash of blood of the interior of her.

At night, the screen doors panels. The couples. low mats. The man with the gentle interior leaning over – the stem out. That had been.

Is there.

Before, the woman with the rim on her gum had fallen drunkenly on the stairs, and hurt herself. Discovered – out – at night – lying – at the foot,

And

the man loping in the street holding – there, very late – bending, the dashes of sweat coming off of him in the dark. As he trots on the street before it.

It takes a long time. But compacted. The screen doors panels at night – the gentle serene interior of the other man, and the others, his stem out – leaning over, at night. It is only, forward,

> that is not at
> all – to be adjusted
> to

The cab goes – feeling shot, in early morning by store fronts small ones with billboards – trash – on the street – and there, paying him the tip contemplating it I don't know what to do give. There. saying the cabby tough what do you want to do not caring.

Riding, came into a small town at night and it was adobe walled completely dark.

> it is
> forward

Light on that ocean but from a cove.

The circumstances of her dying among the pans of oil.

Caught by the man who'd been in the café – as simple as that, which imitates the motion, but isn't the function.

He hadn't intended to kill her but he couldn't leave her a witness – as he was found by her in the domed garage. Four red scratches were raked from his neck down his chest; which he covered with his shirt and suit. Throttling her and then her lying streaked with the oil.

She resisted furiously – him imitating the function.

The steely-blue-eyed man had had his throat cut and that would be known – driving through the valley – if he were in the garage.

If this is the same as the mystery and many or anyone can do it, living freely.

o James Brown – it's said he's in a car chase with the police, with a shotgun – over him busting up an insurance meeting in a building, and now is sent to prison. James Brown. There's no point in arguing any more says the lawyer.

love to him.

The newspaper, only, says – James Brown sentenced to six years after failing to stop in the chase, the pursuit is in ten to fourteen vehicles

last night
it is too difficult

The ocean with the dark grey clouds claps of thunder a sheet of lightning in that night on the lava that is in the waves.

And that is the soft green hills on which the lovely cattle stand here and there that is attached to the lava fingers under the sheet.

The red dirt of the roads on the green – a cloud of the red dirt offshore in the ocean – is not under the sky claps of thunder and sheet of lightning clouds. That are that night.

Ocean grey mass. Stowing away, having watched the deck, and sneaking on up the gangplank. Being in the cardboard box. The freighter, rolling in the heavy swells grey mass of the bulk of grainy water

———————   ———————   ———————

Not locking into it, that being fragile.

I read a book on Dean – *General* Dean. And I was young, eleven and did a report – him in the ditches, manure.

Came in the taxi there'd been a storm here and don't talk enough to the taxi driver.

he's so warm

She was a waitress; who were from the farms working at no minimum. come in to town and the white-haired woman in charge is kindly caring for them there – and one can not live at that his dream observing

The women were chosen, and training by the disciplined matronly coach they ride in the bus through the waste dust bowl flat small houses in the vast terrain to the games where they do the pom-pom. The dust from the bus wake – going on the road behind it.

(I'm) in the car on the road – behind it.

The boys – say – sh-maa-faa – low lilting slurring that is not obscene – dipping in or skimming it. it is wonder or seeing an event or observing – and – may be – that – at the same time

they say that to each other

who're friends

sh-ma-faa

The bus of the game going through the waste – with the dust wake – the car goes behind it, so that there are two dust wakes.

Another one, school bus, intervening on the dirt sparse trees plain, children get out on it. they get out in nowhere. That bus stopping for them to get down – and the car is behind it.

The Pearl

FOR TOM WHITE

On rings over sawdust — holding onto the rings, and changing flying across above the sawdust.

Go into office having been sent for — and ushered in — sitting in the deep leather armchair.

The plain stretching away from the sawdust — on which on the plain in the far distance groups playing a few isolated all along through to that area.

She asked We wondered why you don't speak What are you thinking? It's fine but we just wondered. And throughout saying nothing.

Wandering home, the cars pouring up the street where crossed — with a note pinned to the chest of not speaking.

Wandering alongside the pouring cars.

Not ever speak in the situation, and sent home with the note on one's chest.

They choose a person to be the ballerina, who then dances in the white tutu, and is the conception of the popular social, field on a plain. Which they know, before.

Not chosen — two people are made the office attendants, which is coveted — it is known who are friends. These are the friends, who're chosen. Not to be with one's friends. Those in charge say not speaking has this result of exclusion.

They formed this.

Groups are being chased — seen far off — running chased in order to be kissed and into the far end of the field. Down in it — the thought coming I will always be myself.

So will the cars pouring – whether or not they have been repaired – not the same, running. Coursing on the overpass above the café. The people going into the café, and sitting drinking. An illuminated sky is above them and the terminal.

Those things are living.

Trees wildly living seeming to whirl jutting out sideways from a mountain with the ocean lapping it.

Knowing who are friends, they choose the three friends to do an act. With others also acting or something with their friends. The two friends are attendants to the other one who's the main as the conception, of the popular social. Not on ability. As all the people have.

Wandering home. The cars course up the street. Crossed.

The people sitting, who pour out of the terminal and into it. And near-by the café, is a house which is open in which the fashionable leaves are painted on the ceiling-rim. The house has been redecorated and leaves no space in which there could be books. The people in it not reading. People there not reading.

Working as a chimmy-sweep so that one is on the roof, here and there. A clear sky. Out. Yet the soot sickens the cells, lying in bed with the cells filled with that.

In great pain – in the one's flesh.

The housewife, in one house, looks at the filthy one who's come from cleaning chimmys and is shocked at their doing that.

And yet the soot gets into all the cells, lying in bed, permeates the flesh. Not moving, from being ill.

Not liking jobs, anyway.

Quit that.

A man comes into a room, out, who's dying of the illness many of the men in the city have. He's fairly young. Thirties. He's sensitive lost a lot of weight. He lies down on the sofa – used to think of being acutely aware in dying but in the exact moment of it but that doesn't matter.

Walking, birds fly over so that their bellies are seen.

So if it doesn't have to be the exact moment – and the cars coursing on the overpass by the café. To it.

One of the men flees school. He's sick of it, disappointed. And there being a war.

He goes to live in the desert, with his wife. They buy reddish white-faced calves, but they name them.

The cattle are to be slaughtered. They graze on the sparse shrub lime-green dotted on the waste range.

Visiting him – going out at night to there in the truck.

He makes dope in the ravines wrinkled rivulets like cotton tufts in the sides of the ravines.

To live.

Yet is on drugs, in going to slaughter the first known-steer. They do it. The couple crushing the steer's head. Slitting its throat, with the blood coming from the light red throat.

And the flesh.

And he speaks of seeing the steers look at him. He doesn't kill any more of the cattle. Living out there in a trailer in that heat – with them the cattle on the waste range.

The artery is the freeway – overpass – and the terminal that is near the café. The cars coursing.

Just for those single individuals.

Farmers come into the city which is completely separate. Having lost their farms, are poor.

Lost – themselves there, some ill. Though many on the street who're not ill.

The markets open of the city to which many congregate to pick up things.

And some coming from the city, to that.

The farmers coming in cannot get married. They have nothing. Coming in from the country, they see themselves, in public.

Sitting in a restaurant, among people – a woman obviously referring by nuance to herself says about the other woman that she had been unable to (rather than 'wouldn't') speak, a confidence given to the former, from being ill and unconscious.

Which isn't realistic, of that woman. Who'd wandered home, the cars coursing by.

Though it is said to the others there to describe the former herself. And is there of *her*.

Boys have been knocked from their bicycles, and the bicycles taken from them in the street.

This is by the mass open market of the city.

The (other), who'd wandered – goes to a warehouse to see, and opening the vast sliding doors – there is the empty space of racks and racks of the bicycles standing having been taken from the unknown numbers around of the boys.

Some not identified.

And the cops supposedly cracking the ring. Says the newspaper.

Trucks come into the farmers market at night, in the luminous dim lamps. Unloading crates. The burly sinuous drivers worked.

The (other) has a job simply. She follows a truck the many lines caravan pulling out. In the line, the trucks.

Seen from back. At night. The canvas-covered trucks rumbling slowly. A strand out on the highway.

Out in the country – it's hard, because the truck is now solitary – parked on the side, on a dirt road.

It's quiet – the motor off.

She finds in the tire marks – behind it – a boy lying like an animal to the side in the ditch.

He's dead. He's a child. The sinuous shadowed driver dumping him before pulling off, in the country.

We can't see ourselves – as being from the country. The cops from the city –

She drives – at night, a truck is behind her. The (other) pulls wildly into a gas station. Standing wildly, asking directions. The man black in the lamp answers calmly looking up from crouching.

The trucks are filling here. Out. The sinuous drivers moving amongst the cabs. The man, filling, answering her is very still.

As if he were in hiding, amongst them. Fearing for his life.

It seems.

She gets back into her car, walking back amongst them to it. They are still, though moving. No voices.

Away in the car – driving fast, frightened. And in the morning, the country cops speak to the attendant. Who says he had pumped gas at night.

The addiction that it's simplistic, and that that's accurate. In the newspapers. The books carry views of people, descriptions of these farmers. very literal. In those, realistic. She read in a small bookstore. The girl at the counter is thin

> confused with coming in
> from there

Illness is not in her manner yet confusion of that age. She's sensitive and gentle.

The cars crowding on the streets, crushed, streaming. Sitting, (the other) in her own place.

The (other) woman had remembered ants entering a plant – she'd had – and then right then ants entered her present plant seeing them, poured into it.

That had been a beautiful – this is such a – plant.

She pours water onto it, which she'd done before. The ants rush out, millions a cloud, running on the edge. They run on the leaves.

She is young. She speaks to a lanky swinging moving man somewhat older. He's a driver. He drawls making fun of her. On the corner – she sees him – he's meeting the girl who worked at the bookstore.

rare books.

Seeing the somewhat older thirties woman, who was the former (one) describing herself in speaking of the (other) as if revealingly. A large rear. Acid. Giving off a perfume. acting – as if she is weak.

The former speaks of the farmers as inferior. Ignorant. Not knowing they are there she says I found myself with those people, in a situation.

She fawns on the lanky man-driver. Her large rear – and thin in appendages. He does not appear to respond. In the restaurant. Seen.

At dawn, the buyers have already been are at the open market.

The trucks here and there. In the grounds. The lanky man-driver is found, by her the (other), in one of the canvas-covered trucks rutting with a (some) woman.

He ruts. Leaping about, his arms hunched. Putting his stem in, and then takes it out. Without other contact than his stem in her, then. With her. So that he comes from that, jerking around.

She comes in his withdrawing. Or really when he has.

So that it is past it.

The manager banging on the side of the truck and saying What's the problem. The man-driver goes to the canvas screen, holding it aside. And speaks to him. The manager has them get out.

It's dawn.

Dawn with the corrugated pink clouds in the endless sky with the city. The man had said No problem, meaning there is not that to the manager. Yet stepping down from the truck.

The people may stand in the light.

And read aloud to someone the picture has to be described or seen and then what the figure in it says read.

So it's private.

Dirt of the fields where it had been in the country – where the boy'd been – in the tire tracks of the road. Yet endless unvaried range of the dirt. Fields of it.

The flat road going by.

Then coming to the filling station – out there.

The boy'd been hit on the head. Highway, not there, against purple mountain range – and only – bicyclists in the racing clothes spread out forward on the highway with some stragglers yet a column with force there. Passed occasionally by the cars.

The thick legs of the bicyclists, passing right beside level with their hams legs. The phalanx. Or column.

Of them.

Yet out on the flat dirt fields. The bicyclists had been going up the mountain range, passing them – level, hunched. This is completely separate flat dirt range of fields. She takes her car to be repaired, as living.

Do not act as if it is looking at something

A machine, and so it is the same – as the attendant crouching isn't inclined to work on it.

Not trust mechanics – there are no sweet mechanics –

Yet being able to take the work, and he seems still – as if he's asking supposedly on the job as to the car repair but doesn't hear. Junk, wrecks in the pit-stop where the trucks had come. Which is minuscule. Out there.

> taxi cabby'll fix
> her car in the evening

She speaks to the newspaper man and he has that attitude of things being simplistic without depth and false. that is. He's in his office, littered, and is chain smoking.

the view that people are lackeys fawning or their behavior as the opposite of that then corrupt.

they either do what he says are chumps or they're corrupt in someone else's

The little thin girl at the bookstore had described him there.

The comic book removing and devoid

thinks they'd the thin girl'd not be able to understand. Who're *in* the literal descriptions.

But she will, girl who'd had a flower in her hair as if a flower child. There. The (other) sees her standing swaying in a truck on the outside of a rally. A farm demonstration in the city. The truck moves away, before she's close.

---

city – gangs – and saying Cook, rather than serving You don't have to be the maid all the time. And they were offended.

on a horse, being held in the arms of an older girl, going into a field – the one who'd elsewhere not been speaking.

It not having to be the exact moment of dying in which that one is aware that doesn't matter.

---

on a fence, with others, looking in immense flaccid spread sow with her litter rising braying roaring and a man running up the hill afraid they've gotten in with it. Only *they'd* seen that.

In the center the people on the beach a few at the edges three or so men lying of one the knees up black or fairly purple against the clouds. Others stand, at the rim of shining water and some out in it.

One of the men, travelling – just on – the airplane, goes to sleep dying without waking so he doesn't know and the people companions are badly shaken, only. And his wife at home, never seeing him again.

His ashes are sent back.

Someone saying that this is – popular – and so destructive. There are no actions. And being narrow, – their, that person – before.

Their – the people on the beach.

The young (other) woman goes to see the former of large rear and thin appendages – she is in the aerobics gym among the machines bicycles people on running belts and lifting at the inactive-machine with weights.

People running on the street – city.

The former had been found working frantically. Driving, the (other) goes past the large plate lighted windows on the street here and there throughout with benches and the muscled men working out. In pelts, like wrestlers. In some costumes. The bars near-by, or dead windows of store-fronts there.

– necessarily –

The gentle flower child shows an understanding of the man-driver. Who's, in something, out in the country blowing off sound of fire shooting with milling rows of beer bottles in a party of very young girls and their male friends.

Disconcerting blasting of the guns at the beer bottles.

The sun glancing on the column of bicyclists, who're even.

> as the named-steer
> had been
> slaughtered by someone

The newspaper man has done a story about one of the city's prime-movers – abusing him. It's authority – constructing in the city, contracts. And favors.

Then he calls her up. You're all I've got. Whining. Obviously manipulating.

Only, then the (other) seeks the information, from the cops, and finds that it is the flower child who has been found. A truck driver on the lonely expanse toward the desert ravines of the drug growing they say, had picked her up. She is wrapped in a carpet, beside the road dead, the driver not having known who she is obviously she's just some anonymous.

they say – so the newspaper man's manipulating really fearing – ? – afterwards? – or before?

But it's some other. He's hard drinking in a bar, when she gets to him.

they're corrupt and you're in that – if you don't – manipulating – do – something for him – which is the realm of the man whom he's abusing he constructs, constructing in the city and he is such. They are. He's vicious.

Then he says the opposite – she's on his side – part of his

The people at the rim of the bar. The lanky man-driver not here consuming very curiously. extrapolating.

At the funeral of the flower child, the corpse is on a pyre with the strings of the orange flowers on her her ashes to be put in the river, delta of the bay. Of the poor who put the whole bodies in the river at night not able to afford for burial but that doesn't matter.

that is not the matter.

The lanky man-driver is by the pyre, wearing a white suit. He is still, though moving – as there are people grinding with a camera they think it is a hippy burial who're *themselves* from the city. He lunges at them, without any voice, so that they move.

I hate – jobs – are nothing. Working having to as a dishwasher – went into a café, for coffee and seeing a sign for a job asking the man right away and he said Have you ever washed dishes before?

And goes in early in the morning, dark out, and the waitresses and bus boys are seated Who are you – the dishwasher, a small person – working, heavy lifting, without sitting down or resting or eating

their view. so that one struggles ceaselessly to reverse and undo being – and then they define that backwards into being again.

there is not such, and then that is defined as it

to be released by objectivity that is convention – is defined

the opposite that is convention

just have the mind struggling – even the reason, what is that, struggling on the surface – with itself

struggling on a surface, with itself, which is convention

to a very simple – surface – just give that up. Not go back into this but having given it up before – Now. So there is no struggling at all.

                    the social being
                    from inside itself
                                        can be approached
                                        calm

the one who hadn't come in – this job – had been a boy using cocaine. he was fired. so he could do this

the city filled with this

She has to clear all the tables. A waitress dumps backed-up plates as she's working into the filled sink Are you going to wash or not? The tables throughout are filled with the debris.

never sitting or resting, on her own morphine – from her flesh.

and the boys doing this – throughout the city – in the restaurants – inside.

You sit – and it's just that – just sitting. Not – doing – something. There are not actions

and walk through the people on the beach the black knees or back against the clouds. The shining water is on one side.

In public, (some) on a skateboard go by to the side.

There's a race that's in the main streets and the bicyclists columns going with force the heavy legs the crowd in the street which is filled with bicyclists.

It is inside.

Out there. She goes and finds the dead body of the former woman with the thin appendages – is that as simply. Out there as being *too much*. The woman has a blue throat and face, yet choked. Rigid. She's in a restaurant, as it happens – since she owns it (some) restaurant.

The cops – also – say the filling station attendant is curiously dead as if he's hanged himself in his place in that dirt fields – refueling – they don't believe that.

The wire metal trays – heavily filled – the flatware in trays under the water having to be shaken. The men who're cooks working around.

friends come in.

shaking the trays the flesh hurting, then going out clearing a table.

The lanky man-driver had been out by a lake, naked loaded, jumping around. Making the families across the lake who're out angry. He jumps around from on the rock – not them.

there were other men there – one in the water

boys working in these sweat shops – all over – not related to that, there isn't a relation.

I saw this UPS truck go by and I thought I could do that it

more than this, and I want to know what death is since that's what we are and he says it isn't. it isn't

that's not the matter.

she's speaking to him in a bar and he's saying that's stupid it isn't.

and I worked as a dishwasher that for years and it wasn't hard

He'd worked as a dishwasher –

The lanky man-driver is the father of the flower child.

Out there. Out – riding the cabby says he thinks it's the wire and he's going to come and fix the car that evening.

Things are out there. The people walking in the part of the town – stands. Men in convertibles, just resting not speaking to each other still in the parked convertible.

She's in a bar, and a game is going on on a field working in thirty-below weather with the men crashing into each other in the freezing and their passing the pigskin which is slick and freezing hardened.

By the bar, the freeway overpass makes a bridge under which cars park in which people sleep.

under the bridge and there're people in them. Maybe living in them. Not seen. Walking.

A car ruby-colored is without its doors or roof-hatch there – having been there – only – a while.

She walks home, to the apartment. The walls are thin, the man in the next compartment showering. bumping the wall.

On the pyre with the orange flower garland in her apartment. And him on his pyre orange garlanded in his apartment.

Below her floor, a man plays a cello. He's played many nights.

The man of the funeral pyre garlanded bumping against the wall. Urinating at night.

Reading – happy.

The newspaper man calls up. She's corrupt – in that. They're in – such. Putrefying. A horde a vast – favors – of groupies and lackeys. and –

Yet, what is it –

She goes to lunch with the man in constructing – in a windowed place on Market St. Had slid down the grass hills, getting in the cardboard box and going down it. The man has contracts of course with the truck lines.

The former, woman who'd then owned a restaurant had been his secretary some time ago.

holes pulled out in the city that are the debris of the inner city. and the walled pillared thin facaded buildings are implanted in that

The (other) had found the former, lying on the floor. All the bottles glasses are thrown. Though not at the woman.

The person'd begun throwing coming in.

And her connection to the man in constructing is what, who's found dead on a pyre that's floating in the water near the Port. he's as if soused as if drink had been poured on him high alcohol in his blood and him floating on the pyre.

Through the night, of when they'd lunched.

In the morning, she went down to the Port the guernes and the cops have their cars out on the dock. The gulls coming cruising in, strong. Attracted.

The important builder. Now the cops are going to be really in this. The mayor has spoken to the press and expressed her shock.

And they're on her the (other) questioning about the thing sitting in the office. Downtown. She'd lunched with him

murdered about five and put out there

and he doesn't go back to his office in the meanwhile.

then gets in the cardboard box and shoots down in it on the hill on the heavy thick long grass.

It is not on ability—as they have that. though or what is that—?—a construction, that is hollow isn't actual. There could be working a machine and that is an ability they have. and isn't actual.

———————

The man who showers in the compartment next to her shouts at her. He's out in the street turning in sitting in his car.

And how could she hear him yet it happens she hears and opening the window—he's shouting her name, he's hit a dog is upset and wants to use her garage.

there aren't parking usually for many blocks on the street

Night comes and the windows are all open

many in the compartments. A girl is in an adjoining basement that floods. She drinks, and wanders drunken.

There's a scream from her side and he comes out from his in a wild roar as the man emerges from the driveway in it squealing

There, the man filling station attendant who'd supposedly hung himself—not believing that—he's not into their, though refueling, out in the dirt—who cares for them who'd gotten him? Their actions—

there are no sweet mechanics. and they must have strung him catching him when he's crouching working. An emerald green colored car with tools beside it and one heightened on the rider who commits suicide while they're working?

And that's out there.

His brother says why is she doing this – though he's still – not in to this – as their – as neither are. how to get them and not be part of it – for him.

Walking with him, seeing that. Just going out there, where there isn't anything – the car lots on either side for sale so that there aren't houses – the low passing jumping cars throbbing stopped at the light there. Or somewhere with him.

Strip.

Yet in the area where there are people – are some strolling, some holding babies.

Yet the man is deft – he's not saying – and she doesn't know what he'll do. of course.

that's before these other two deaths anyway – the man lying on the pyre floating

She's out interviewing the people who live in trailers and are defective and they don't pick up on their guarantee they don't complain so the government for consumers wanting to know why

they aren't getting good living quarters

and they say they can handle it

why don't they complain they say they can handle it It isn't other's business. They're hostile and they don't want to file a complaint.

That's them. it's raining their trailers leaking.

And she stops in the rain because the sunset's in her eyes and has four drinks on a highway.

they say they don't want any charity

he isn't saying that he doesn't care about that he doesn't care what they say.

----

the form of the comic book so
it doesn't matter

                    the self – that's the
                    same form

This was said earlier than (this). There wouldn't be a sense of time.
                    there – is no – future
This is arbitrary – was.
So that repression would not be a way of giving depth.

that isn't really so – the girl is still. And is found by a man unknown to her
who was driving, with her wrapped in a carpet.

   just the slight body – flesh – so that it is inside the carpet, dead not her, left
to the side of the road in the desert.

                    this is for no
                    purpose – free

Why would you think that there wouldn't be unusual – when someone
dies – it is. they're doing something.

   why would you think they're not doing something

Shaking the flatware in the trays under the water, the flesh hurting. The
mayor says that children are runners for drugs – and she the mayor doesn't
connect this to the important builder, who's mourned officially.

   The (other) goes to the city dinner and ball. This is not the wake – it's planners.

   Yet the lanky man-driver is there and getting into a fight with someone –
far off.

   She dances with him and he leaps, the (other) whirls around him as if a
top. His eyes are gently slanted downwards as if contemplating.

   ever with an eye for women – has drunk as if it were distilled off of him
and at the same time wiry lanky hunched keenly watching (he's angry – at
them) – and he's dancing like a wiry billy goat.

Get out of the car in the desert – at night – so it's cold, and looking up there are stars in the sky.

but keeping an alert – at something – at the crowd.

the constructor'd had a wake him laid out in one room and (some other dead in another room and the crowd had wandered back and forth through the rooms getting increasingly looped til it was crazy and the lean swerving man-driver was there too

so was she.

Others arriving with the ashes of an other. Outside it's quiet.

When one's father dies, one is – up to death.

Here they're dancing dragging the floor and the constructors foxtrotting fast and suavely. The second-partner assistant constructor is there.

My line drawings are the purest and most direct expression of my emotion. (Matisse.) group, in the very center some slight leaping.

He's running then, far off, and she is also, in mud the dirt fields in heavy beating rain the mud dark it's later that same night. plain the rain beating on it. It's cold. Running, the lining of the lungs is felt. In the dark.

Though nothing can be seen ahead, both get separately to the canvas-covered trucks out there. As they begin to move. There're no people out of the trucks – and he jumps catching on to the outside of a truck riding. She climbs up holding on outside a truck on the back riding. The line of trucks beginning to whirl, the headlights cast over, and get in line.

The trucks stay close together on the highway slowly and in the beating heavy rain, and he wiry hunched leaping runs forward on the top, and the cab and jumped to the separate (some) truck.

He jumps in the heavy rain to another truck. and she on another one clinging gets onto its cab, on her feet jumps clinging to the (other) canvas cover.

He's on the side of a truck clinging to the and crawling and in the window of the cab one of the sinuous drivers is discarded and to the side of the road. And she's dropped and they've gone on the line of them.

stretching flat unvaried mud in the dark, walking on the road in the beating rain. To return. Towards the city. And then the bicyclists that way, col-

umns of them the swish of the bicycles around her force past her and then another column. The swish then of that as she's walking in the dark.

Another column. then. Toward the city.

Returning, the thin wall the man who'd showered near her urinating.

it's not even light the newspaper man calls – she's corrupt – they're – in –
with

birds from the roof just take off brushing her touching her past fast

---

you have to be just that, only

The flower child laid to rest lying garlanded on the pyre, innocent limpid
with no accumulation.

This has no ability – irrelevant – that is not the matter

where is my little pearl fallen
in the ground

the assistant constructor – fragile – controlling – and that has no ability
that is actual. The setting up – facades – boards – in the city.

Weeping.

the lanky man had come in

to the business-like efficient rigid – former who is the function – who'd
come to own a restaurant, had been in the aerobics gym – the people being
here and there in windows with the machines.

yet he finds her in her own business, coming in begins throwing glasses
bottles – to find something out from her.

he's the father of the flower child – he goes to the important builder from
her. But whom he doesn't find. Who's then missing.

I met her on the street near her
and she wouldn't speak to me

The artificial – assistant constructor – finds – walks in – to the empty restaurant – of the woman, and he bruises her. murders, and then goes right to
the builder catching him on the street.

And he lays it. the stiff. so it'll the constructor'll be on the pyre. to be like
the flower child's funeral.

The ants are still in her place trailing on the wall like in a freighter

And throughout in the city – setting that – constructing – wealth

there are no sweet mechanics – the attendant'd been strung from seeing
them.

> the car hers jumping throbbing on the rim
> of the steep hill of the city and
> hanging on it to get to the edge and come
> down on it

The day so clear and beautiful, when the car's hanging on the rim.

> to do it this strip and never to do
> anything else on

and checking into the motel unlocking it and the made bed and crude art
on the wall and the sink in the motel bathroom. Washing her face.

Going.

the car whirls, kicking up some dust. in turning. just flat, cars going.

A plan to turn over part of the state oil monopoly to the private sector was
the "political cause" behind the arrests, a senior government source said yes-
terday.

> what is a newspaper what is
> that she wondered

> the cars vans perched in the yard neighboring
> of the people who eat in their window
> at the table inside with their cars floating on the
> dewed grass

the beauty of the light blue dusk sky so
this is not the matter

Standing on the corner at night under the lamp and in a phone booth – but
it does not have doors – and a man when no one else is there comes bran-
dishing a club twirling coming close and then backing off again.

so she says I must go now.

What was with him. could have wondered that but didn't.

he's a solitary dream

and so leaving no space. With half-shaved head and swinging the baseball
bat. He moves forward and then back. And forward.

Moon and clouds travelling over it. And she's back in her apartment when
a cop arrives. She hasn't called.

leaving no space
and letting them come in to it

The man wearing short pants and had a partly shaved head – alert is not
the matter.

Saw when I was walking the sun at the bottom of the hill, a large dark red
oblong distorted ball resting at the foot of the hill.

the street went right down the hill – and at the bottom was the huge red
dark sun.

It is doing something.

Raised, on the bike – still, on the rim of a hill, now not in the car

people batting the ball on the court with the
palace Claremont Hotel behind them whang and
she's standing watching them outside – in the evening

The whirr of the bike, yet it is the flesh. mounted on it. Had seen the races
on foot in the streets of the city in such heat they were fainting enervating.

And one runner staggering wandering unwilling or forgetting to stop past it while she is in public wanders behind the few.

    that was going to finish – hurting the mind – and the horde of the athletes running

> that is not the matter to
> not hurt the mind

    A child comes into a shop with others, hovering. Barely notices him, and then someone in the shop says are they after you to the child – of the other children – yes – and they're waiting til he goes out of the shop on the street.

    A man speaks about the crescent moon hanging above the bridge – he says this in the conversation.

> people don't do it in
> conversation

He hangs in there speaking seriously of the moon

    and she goes into a small market and tries out for them minute, working all through the day at the cash register – the customers – only vegetables – open – yet the man not asking her to come back at the end. It is in the center.

> not have anything
> happen in
> there

    The (other) works in a yard and with dirt smudged on her clothes walks through the town home. In one area the people pouring clapping they're in rush of the construction – fraternities, sororities – from far off, and the (other) is amongst them.

    you're corrupt or you're weak – someone else's – a function – says the newspaper man to her

    – a function and receiving

a man who's out in the area of the vegetable market's – free – crouching receiving clapping in the construction – walking

the form but now no longer the
same in it

then going out on the road the dirt flats – the flesh mounted. Standing, yet
on the bicycle. It's night dark a column the swish of them around her past toward the city.

Another column. Returning. The whirr the heavy legs even, touching her
going past.

Some standing here and there, balancing on the ground.

On the highway. Cars go past.

Dirt fields away. A woman-of them to the side counting her money which
is knotted tied in her clothing, is pausing to one side of the others.

And one lying in the dirt field others. amidst. nude utterly relaxed. an arm
is thrown back.

A man – in that group. his stem out, standing.

A thinned out column. Then. Of the bicyclists ahead. Toward the city.

Coming through slowly walking having come from the hill and smudged
with dirt – walking amidst the clapping people who happen to be doing that.
They put their arms in the air clapping doing a ceremony of the rush and she
is going right through them slowly an anomaly there.

The dirt of the hill.

Not grazed by that grazing it the person in the cardboard box going down
over the shimmering heavy long grass regardless of him later being dead –
having slid down the hill's side then.

she sees a man weeping for his little daughter who's gone now fallen in the
ground, going past.

walking – yet out there and then lying since on the sea having a leaf and
her flesh is purple on the huge ocean with just that water. The emerald green
leaf and the purple being on it.

love – just loving – beforehand – openly

a part of The Pearl

She's in her apartment, and gets a call hiring her for a job or trying to. She has to see first.

They come on over. They want him to have protection. Not very forthcoming – about it – though about other aspects.

They want him to be accompanied – he's afraid. He's grey-haired incredibly handsome he gets right down on the bed sitting back as if he were lying with his face up.

there aren't many chairs in the place.

The woman's a friend in a black nylon dress and a fox stole really, from a used store and is an aging cheer-leader having a wonderful way of beginning to say something, and then turning and moving away as not to continue in that conversation.

doesn't stay bored.

with him who talks and that is just acting.

in saying that – so that there is the chance that someone hearing it feeling will repeat that. Saying just action to someone else. though he isn't.

anyway she doesn't know about this.

In the evening she goes over to a café with booths. People are out selling flowers at the vendor – there are parties – and he's at that and then she can't find him.

Through the windows and people's gardens seeing them holding glasses a party continuing. Out beyond are the backyards fences – though it's night.

The flower child is dead.

She walks slowly through the garden.

He's lying there a kind of lout handsome face staring up. Frightened she bends over to hear his chest, he's breathing his eyes open. He's like a lotus. He's all right. drunken.

Having – he'd called really late one night – gone all the way across town to give him valium as he'd mumbled on the phone.

He'd needed it. he says on the phone.

He's heavy tall and not possible to lift him – a small person, yet she drags him. The night is dense – a magnolia tree with the purple tinged white blossoms is still, unfolded in it.

He'd said I'll need your car – I'll be expecting to use it – and then, It won't be necessary, someone else had

given him their car.

the lout handsome face lotus body dragged. Barely, getting him into his car – and she goes through his pockets for the keys.

Not there. It's cold – she's stuffed the lotus sack heavy onto the back seat out dreaming presumedly.

And goes on. near-by. The groups are breaking up of the parties a few people out on the neighboring streets. a woman squatting to urinate in the gutter at the side of the street.

running – going by ditches in the evening with
frogs in them

other people coming out from a house go by.

she falls asleep. Being inside an empty exposed house the back window broken no locks on the back or front doors. It's very cold, freezing. the (other) gets into a bedroom which is the only door which locks.

at 3 there's tapping banging and getting up leaving the locked room without considering – still – turning on the light in what is the living room.

– only – action and it
is open

coming in – she'd drawn the curtain – early.

something leaps up onto the back porch. A dark shape of a girl with another girl hanging behind her. They have been running – through the gardens.

They look up at the broken window, seeing there is no help.

say they've been hiding in gardens – get down and crouch in a garden, and then move on. Men are following them, who'd stop meandering in the car while a man searches the bushes.

so there's only one light amidst the block, here.

so they come right there. Beating on the door. She'd been sleeping on the floor in the bedroom. They're crouching now on the floor beneath the (window) – front door – which can be opened. She's standing says go away to the men, and for some reason they do.

Answering something, not knowing. And saying that of not knowing anything about it. And some other says you'd be a person who'd always raise their hand in class. Waving I have the answer, I have the answer.

She walks back across town to her own car. It's miles. The heavy lotus lout is still in his back seat – like a fraternity boy in the back seat of a car. It's not dying, there is not that.

He's soft. His handsome face fell back under the moonlight, as she yanks him the sack.

somehow he's in her car.

more on the
surface – weeping

sack of hop – not caring for himself – and caring very much.

takes off the car going very fast. She's out by the bay, the moon's low bulbous light and there's another car going slow. She gains on it in the lane over. The car moves over going slow 25 in front of her.

Then she's slow behind it. It remains. She moves over to pick up to get past. It moves over slow in front of her.

It remains. She moves over again to the right lane. It moves slow holding in front of her.

Then it takes off. very fast.

And there's this pink sky that's in front but as if – beforehand. To the events (of that night) that entire day goes, and then there's this incredible vast corrugated rungs of rose colored yet extreme sunset as if it had covered the sky and is behind it, pushing.

She's driving up the street of small flat porched houses and it's behind her, and stretching in front as well.

And as if the events are pushed – from it.

What's happened – ? – she'd slept during the day. Checking the man's apartment, he's not there.

Goes over to a bar. The man is there being vicious speaking of some-one's nature to them. He's getting into a fight – after a while – obtusely. The woman fox stole is sitting at the bar, with the particular flapping, in conver-sation – and moving away as soon as she's started one. That is her form love as is evident.

with the people seated. It is a dark blue evening – outside.

the (other) is simply sitting.

Clanging going on. Just clanging inside. Then in Al Hudaidah on the Red Sea having driven all day, in the hotel small humid room like a tank and hole in the wall upstairs through the side of the hotel hall.

it is not there

Yet with time she goes out in the evening and he's lying in the car, checking him he's all right, leaving himself – in the back seat.

a few people are out.

She goes back in.

in a while she's out again and there's a body there – not him – decompos-ing flower of someone. So –

and it's in the car.

The cops examining it – and the turning of the lights on the roof of their car, and it's removed in the cop van.

it turns out this is a dancer

The person who's the director of the company the main dancer describes him but there is nothing that says what had produced the decomposing body – their – only. She's the director doing – this – her husband's there, seated, who's a scientist – very deep direct – attached to each other.

The dancer who's been dead – had been of course young and with initial but strong muscular ability.

not going
to know flesh

and he's died

had fought, been strangled – does not resemble the heavy sack. Who has no memory of this.

Apparently – he's out of the car, drunken wandering down the street. and the cops don't like this.

she has this job.

used to think the social setting as only conformity – could only see that. that was true

When one repeats saying a thing which is just movement, but said to someone, it is contemplating.

The director shows her the other dancers. What's his relation to the bar – he hadn't even been in it.

so they'd just used a still car, out?

to put him in there.

pigs turning on ship deck swaying with its rolling, having mind.

The (other) is at home, showering, standing under the water and the peeling paint of the shower with the mold held in the wall.

Water seeps through from the compartment next to hers at times, also. They don't repair it.

Fresh, she lies down in bed. The man who's behind and beyond the thin wall of the compartment next to her is in bed also—she can tell, he's quiet. She laughs, from reading—and his feet hit the floor a dog barks outside and he runs out shouting if you'd keep the fucking dog in the house this wouldn't happen.

Watching the dancers—the husband scientist watches them—also.— they have a blonde-haired boy—a child—playing near-by. The woman, who's directing, shows them movements.

The actual little lambs on the lighted hill running. Some were kneeling.

the same

Man lotus is in the car behind her in it she's driving.

It's night—the parties people standing inside. A man comes out from the bushes parting them, down from a thickly covered slope.

to one.

The (other) is walking in the dark on the sidewalk, the bushes parted a man steps out. He has a metal hook on his hand instead of the hand. She jumps frightened. so he expresses anger to her had to take a leak in the bushes.

and had to go into the war.

She's inside with people in a lit room with glass patio doors. The hostess and host are in constructing, planners. She sips her drink a few.

And leaving driving him a car goes by glancing them. Slows in front of them

even still

and then she pulls around. And it pulls in front, again. It's not the highway. They're on the quiet empty streets. She manages to go past and take off, fast. L.'s dream:

> they were leaving college and were going to part
> and she wanted to convince him not
> to part were in love which he felt and
> he assumed they would part

yet when she woke he wasn't gone.

The emerald green being on the ceiling – her – having come in from the night – doesn't struggle.

why should it. not struggling.

the green being, and the night outside

Bursting on to the plain before being in Al Hudaidah on the Red Sea there but going toward it clumps of huts in sand or dirt vast colored plastic bags hanging still on tufts of brush and then in the plain.

Dark green trees on the town street hanging over it. and these birds are singing hundreds in the trees.

She walks under them. People are sitting on the sidewalk.

Leaning on a fence, is a hayseed with others. He's arrogant – doctrinaire – haughty to her. From the country. And she realizes she's seen him in one of the parties where he'd crashed. had thrown empty beer cans at someone.

And not having seen the man in the slowing car she realizes it's him.

like looking into the back seat of the car at the lotus body lying there – it's not dead. It's not doing that.

The people seated at the rim in the bar – they're not. She gets really happy, walking – the magnolia tree is not doing anything. She goes over to the sack's apartment. He's not there.

He's outside under a tree, smoking.

bobbing dark heads are just past the surf in the ocean and she is among them. Floating. the limbs floating hanging down into the water.

she goes back along the beach.

he's in the car – only – he's dead, and she hadn't come there with him.

he'd been brought there – to where she is.

The flower child is dead – he is not a flower child.

She drives slowly – bewildered – the man lying in the back. Yet out on the highway – there're cops everywhere – it's in stagnant crush of cars. They're not moving. And she sees hayseed walking among through the cars. He's selling newspapers. She gets out walking brushing the sides scraping past the hot fenders.

               it is not contacted by
               being

a body in her car – and the cops are around

from far back, he's moving as if running to her the hayseed.

Well so she just left the car stopping in traffic with a body in it with cops yes because you were being followed? and the cop leans back accustomed to it.

in his office.

She's failed – badly. They'll be looking for the hayseed, his mouth glinting shining as he drank beer at the bar.

Walking under the dark green trees black in part. And the hundreds of birds singing in them – and the people sitting underneath.

               that was not coming
               from this

The couple who'd been in the party – in constructing – had a job with her client they'd murdered him, rather than the hayseed.

He's the hayseed's employed by them wants to get a little extra from them when he finds what they're doing.

and says he'd dumped the decomposing body – into the fellow's car – having found it.

He says this to the cop.

She's out walking and he is in front of her. And the sun is fiery shining blinding her eyes for a moment as if mercifully saying sleep, so that this could occur. He's doing something.

As if a bird came down.

They're holed up in the gardens people – to get away from the illness that is rampant. And then they are also with each other in conversation.

               imitation doesn't
               matter

Out in the country.

A man standing, puts his stem in through the hole that's in a door. The open exposed places.

The couples.

Hours in the night.

Others sitting. Her. The purple being out lying on the leaf in the ocean.

The (other) can float, and is out, floating. She has a job. A hillbilly hires her wanting her to find his adolescent daughter. He doesn't want her to use any science in this. He believes in the virgin birth, and.

She goes down to Venice beach and walks around. People go by on roller skates. There are—that—and she watches the muscled men lifting their weights there.

they're there

The hillbilly has never met his daughter. He doesn't know where the mother is.

She used to live in L.A. Easy.

> he saw before the
> hill a woman and she held
> his heart—the sun shining in his eyes
> —between them there was love—as if
> saying Sleep, to him so
> that he couldn't keep his eyes open,
> which were separate from him.

The military had killed many thousands. scientist finding by the DNA the babies who had been adopted of the dead parents.

First we'll kill all the subversives. Then we'll kill their collaborators. Then we'll kill their sympathizers. Then their friends and relatives. And then we will kill the timid.

Why did they do that? there was no mercy. is. one doesn't know what to do. There's no relation between the light air and this. merciful city. light as glare. heat. A kind of haze that covers so that can occur. But what had been gentle before. And benign. she's looking for the old neighborhood of the hill-billy's (unmarried) wife.

the athletes had run through the streets one weaving staggering in the intense heat dense in which those the running athletes here that occurring.

> the people standing watching fear that
> she'll hurt her mind
> almost winning

though some other wins.

She's out on the phone on the street in that intense oppressive air. It's for the girl – the man on the phone is cruel, jacking her around. She's in misery, has lost her mind of which he's aware.

> the heart's companion and
> in him

Faceless people in the heat of day pass by. Or she doesn't see them, just them brushing by. To be utterly dependent on him.

> not able to weep – so
> desperate that is
> detached from this

That this is occurring – it occurs to her – it is not dying – so dying seems irrelevant, it is not the matter – rather, what's the substance of this is. The people out and the buds that precede – rather.

> buds on the trees

The man on the phone had said come forward – leading her, jacking her around – why? – in the matter

> before the hill

The person cannot see the inside community – which would be a separation from others – or that is not there. It is not there.

The cop, sitting in his office speaking to her, says this happens always.

She is speaking to the hillbilly, having come to his house going onto the porch. He is sitting in his kitchen and has a wonderful way of throwing the empty beer can so it makes the paper bag on his floor. for the trash.

He aims. the trash bag falls on its side, glanced by the can.

He goes to the window. She follows him. He leaves the window and letting himself down on the roof of the next house, runs across it. Then he gets down on the next roof and runs across that one.

Two men lower themselves onto the next house's roof and come out after them.

They have come through his door.

She drops to the ground from a drain and they continue following him over the roofs without diverting their attention from her companion.

> there is not the relation between it and
> being

so there is calmness, speaking on the phone in that utter extremity is a memory. that was in a morning. and one walks by a black fast-running river or slate-colored the same as the sand.

no features or reflexion – or color – fast-running.

where the salmon enter there, at an other time, from the ocean and begin swimming up it. But the slate-colored river – seen, when she's there – is empty. The utterly wonderful.

One day she sees an older small woman walking slowly, as she has difficulty, up the street by people who are sitting on the sidewalk – who recognize her lovely as one of their own, though she is not in that circumstance. Of being on the street. She is one of them. She is lovely, and going by, she reciprocates their nod to her of recognition.

The dick finds the girl, mother works in the store.

The hillbilly runs and jumping up on a wire fence clings to it looking into a schoolyard where there are children in groups. runs along the fence. clings to the fence holding onto it shaking, and looks in at her.

II

Legs floating back and then forward – and then back. Cruising – going around the ring, with the padded arms and knees that so coming up on – one – elbowing slamming in to get by them.

Round – cruising. And their coming up fast strolling crouched the legs crossing over. the legs floating back, their, and then forward – as they're coming up, slam, and slammed into the wall.

The legs cross over.

Round the ring low strolling crouched – coming up on and elbowing her and to get past them. Slamming into her (another) going by – And cruising.

One bit. Cruising being hit – and she without knowing sinks her mouth teeth deep into – the – lower lip of with the taste of blood filling in a pool having been slammed.

Then withdrawing. The legs floating back, and then forward.

Their roller derby gear by the benches, and the changing rooms. Out afterwards, it's afternoon.

Dream of three separate people who're there who betrayed, one a blasted idiot who I'd never want to see again and in the dream is friendly and had worked a ship coming up the river on a cruiser military in the Sudan as if I should forget grudges yet outside of it I'd never want to see the blasted idiot nor would they again in life.

though seems so warm in reunion with them as if there are friends

This can be free and serene in that it uses itself up. There's nothing left after reading it.

Strolling crouched fast the legs floating back and forward. With, among the group up the street at night.

to be in their view men
who're crouching in a doorway

Walking.

        Coming up the hill in the
        light dusk evening and a dog
        was coming along and
        vomited inside before me

                in the
                dusk air of
                the hill

The joy – that is not related to that.

        light evening dog shyly
        in it vomiting so that it
        is coming along the hill

Waking up the heart racing, lying at night. The panic is because of not living, and yet that is.

Lying, the heart's racing, waking at night from nothing. Fear, panic, which is of not living at all. While in it.

        the dog that had vomited on the hill
        is living

Someone who's a friend and then simply not speaking any more when the usefulness has been used up of one.

Which is amazing why would they do that known deeply so it's up to this surface.

is just that is inside and there isn't any commentary. Or it is the commentary outside – the same.

Riding in the back of the bus and a branch comes in hitting me from the window a scream and the seated others averted their faces embarrassed in the rows before with shame.

I urinated into the different sizes of containers to practice. To have the urine be the amount with the tablet slipped in. And when I was in the toilets at the army I slipped it in they didn't believe I'd be that sick or sick and having me come back to be drafted. I'd practice into the containers with the amounts of the powder in my clothes.

People not liking it and I ran forward bending down for the canister the teargas spewing out threw it back. There was a clearing. With the crowd.

It is fine.

They call asking for Mrs and I say can I take the message and they never learn they never figure it out. Ha ha.

It's hot they're making a living calling and they never figure it out.

Concentrating on the visual.

So that the friend who no longer speaks and people's behavior is turned around is inside and the men on the street crouching grainy in their own view.

Man crossing the street in front of a car is hailed and he rears and then squints forward looking and rears.

Greeting.

They've gotten in to something and were there.

And so because there isn't that event existing.

Waking at night, lying. Rearing from there not being a life.

That there isn't.

III

Forgetting, or not remembering to breathe and then a breath and then not remembering to do it for a time wandering a band seeming to be around the rib cage constricting so that there can't be a breath.

A breath, and not in to the chest. a band constricting so that breath isn't in it.

Trying, and then forgetting to breathe

And then in to or there is serene area, a hole in the hall in the side of the second floor of hotel, in humid small room in Al Hudaidah having driven all day in sand-dust plateau to room and in that.

Not anything there. the utterly wonderful.

The breath isn't in the chest, of the constricting rim of the rib cage. So decided to sleep completely worn out in which there is breath apparently going on though not aware of it.

People seem so mean never caring about anyone how do they cooperate to make a thing though it's there (the thing) and they did it and just stay in this. in this.

They're out screaming and wailing I mean that's a *wake* and I had gone to a florist having a wreath made of fresh flowers something special I brought it and she said Oh I didn't want *those* throwing themselves about I found out, the flowers were dead before we got there and I'm trying to fan them to keep them going laughs

They don't stay in our schools for long, can't stand them. (I don't know why. You just said why.) They're separate. Children being taken away from their home by an agency, and they can't find or see them. A long conversation-monologue on their separate sense of reality.

Then in to – sitting in a car on the desert seeing a woman – other who's in stopped car commenting This one is about forty They age so and There are many deaths; the speaking doesn't matter – get out from pickup truck to grave yard to place wreath plastic flowers are on the crosses by the road, and in her, walking to plot on sand floor where there's nothing in the town of drag strip with taco stands and car lot condominiums

Of the constricting band of the rib cage, or not. Breath in chest. Woman out on desert looks up with irritation at observers and places the plastic flowers.

There're these ugly towns to come to that are flat box facade by drag strip and stands the planes coming over from the base in the sky and where there's a yard with the 40's planes dumped standing as the elephants' graveyard or 50's a dump. To get in there. They sit in lines and lines, taxiing.

Anyone.

Very hot breath coming from outside. Up in crate, looking down.
uh – uh – uh uh – uh uh – uh uh uh uh – that's its sound, of artillery

You don't
know
anything
about war

Nothing at all

I was dancing with him saying he's going to be a race car driver so I say this to the other boys when we're back to the side from the floor and I'm to have another partner and they say he doesn't know anything about race cars he wouldn't know any more about race cars than

You're not listening,
You can't listen while you're talking

Oh I don't know. Maybe I can

One has a dream of oneself sitting on a knoll. Down in the valley, some gentilhommes are going by carried in sedan chairs, a winding dirt road. Coming close, approaches them, those who're carrying them bent. One greets them. They do not answer. Running after them who're carried in the sedan chairs.

With the sweat pouring down the body. 'One had loved them.' One doesn't not love them. Their not wavering, those carrying them swaying slightly sagging bent. On the slope.

In a large room, where there is going to be a reading. Sitting on a red pillow in the center – the walls are lined with gentilhommes seated who do not nod to one though knowing them. A man was seated on a pillow next to one, who begins pushing jostling to force the person off the red pillow.

They're around who look as if why doesn't she know what or where she should be, yet holding with her hands to the edges of the pillow so as not to be pushed from it. The man knocks her until she rolls onto the floor off of the pillow. Their faces, in the center, are retentive, hostile – as are the men's along the wall.

On the hard floor, having rolled. Yet when there is a man going up and reading, it is the man who had knocked her off of the pillow, in the center.

He smirked. Addressed as he begins in greeting by a man, he rebuffs him as not knowing him. who rebuffed waits for a few moments and then leaves the assembly. As the other is reading.

A blonde man flick of the head hesitating – as they are known to one – wave of the faces of those sitting along the wall in not speaking in stupidity of gentilhommes.

Though that's a mystery – knowing that's stupidity, yet they're doing it.

She has no car. A man who lives in Berkeley is there so she asks him for a ride, and on the bridge over the bay driving in the lights night he's burly light, at the wheel, saying it's just clubs. Though it had not been spoken of between them.

She's in her room afterwards in the dark and weeps.

not coming from that

They were to get up at midnight to go to the airport and she had been put to bed in the meantime. Waking, she was fully dressed having done that herself and was tying her shoe, crying very loudly. She had done this in her sleep. The person is empty. says Why am I crying, and stops.

A sister is dressing in the same room looking at her with sympathy because she is crying – the person is also empty but extends empathy to her. And she notices that. At that age.

Weeping when waking while tying the shoe – the men sagging swaying as they carry the sedan chairs on the slope, and breathing. Which is the comic book.

being inside itself – so it's the same as that, and so it can't come out can't come out – of what – ?

as is the occurring of the being rolled onto the floor off the pillow – the man climbed onto it. Which doesn't matter. Those in the room won't speak because they have to have that.

that's why one weeps

to give them that, which is irrelevant

To receive sympathy doesn't matter at all – one would ask for sympathy bullying someone outside of the setting there and as a means of doing so so the men extended the sympathy to him who was asking them for it. He is weak – what is weak.

He would go after bullying one in a gathering and seeking approval in that as needing sympathy which is extended to him.

I don't know.

The muscles ripple up the arm of the man. Whose arm quivers rippling as he was speaking to her, at a gathering. pow on the side of the head and she reels from it.

So seen them carried, far away on the slope – so one runs to catch up. Slipping on the slope. Long yellow grass, with very blue sky above it. On the slope.

Those who're carrying the sedan chairs breathing, sagging.

Scrambling down the yellow slope – in the blue sky.

There's nothing to do. The slope ahead is then charred black a hill that has burned. Stubble – black slope, running across it.

Hill that is in the future, which is the comic book

That's not accurate.

When she was behind. The buzzards careening above the long yellow grass.

low gutting – it was like an elephant in the ocean.

The buzzards whirl.

trunk extended.

warbling.

Having before been on the black charred hill.

Seated across from the blonde man in a café – who'd extended himself as sympathy for the one who bullied – he is speaking as if speaking to her. But not valuing – which is convention.

The comic book. And so it is nothing.

He wants her to do a job.

Trying to learn anything in any circumstance – is caring what people think, and so is nothing. It occurring to one I will have to do this myself – and felt a sense of joy.

what is this

this is not double going at the same time – though they like it

The blonde man in the café pretending to speak to her – not valuing, as convention, is all right. And he extended – sympathy – to the man who's the bully, who is his alliance.

When the tanks came in and shot and mowed over in the crowd. A man with a bird cage passing by on the street. He began cursing the soldiers in one tank, for being animals. Standing in front of them. And pow they shot him in the chest like a flower.

The comic book is calm.

That's why this must be nothing and see it is that. That it is nothing – in a way. When it's through, it's simply disappeared – there isn't anything left of it.

Then we're not saying. that doesn't occur. There are not senses before the yellow slopes.

It is going before or ahead of this, here.

Out one day, by the highway exit ramps.

The men working on the street were nearby – with their banners, orange on frames.

She walks by the mounds of dirt. and whang muscles rippling up the arm of the man off who's to the side – not among the mounds – to the side of her head. It rings, her reeling.

The man working in the mounds comes out. They're going to have a fight with the one who bullies.

speaking to him, who says demagoguery – and pow to the side of her head, as they're standing there. In a cluster. The men with their banners up in the road want to protect her.

But this isn't needed – for there are only good intentions in anyone ever.

saying someone else's action, which may be occurring for the first time, is contemplating.

In the trench, of the cut dirt. crouching.

The arms out whirling the wheel, caterpillar rearing tearing down street by row of trench.

Cluster of men from the mounds, on the corner.

Bearded driver whirling wheel, tears around corner and comes again – caterpillar by trench the mounds are along the way – scanning fast for the man who's the bully, not the (other).

The open seat of the caterpillar racing
mounted seat of it rearing tearing

is occurring for the first time. and so there is no life.

Their orange banners on frames – hold in the street.

bearded face peering out sideways on mounted – going by – in back of coverage of the blossoms.

Then moon in the sky.

The man'd been in a group on one night and the others had poured out sympathy to him.

Having asked for it – as someone else's action.

The other is sitting under a magnolia tree

> and pow to the side
> of her head

it reels – in the night where they are. No one exists and that is not the matter.

She goes down to the corner. It isn't a matter of time – for there does not appear to be change.

Later the blonde man in the café speaking to her knows he is pretending and she knows that – he extends sympathy to the one.

that is not convention.

she had read the letters of the one sent filled with wanting to humiliate some other utterly.

if he's not going to be speaking then where is he

In the night light the straightened limbs jump into the air – under the overpass of the highway, the ball dribbling the limbs spring.

he wants her to find someone (else) for him, who she does find.

The limbs straightened go up, the ball arches and goes in – the limbs go down, here and there.

The men jump up

The jasmine giving off a scent

The women are sawing on the violins out of which burst the flow – rows in the house with the flow pouring.

arm goes up, in the night – straightened leap – and the ball dribbling
the limbs up and then down, here and there.

The violins their going on them – and then an oboe that is below the
flow – doing there, caught
the women hold out from the throat of one the flow, that is just on it
and then the row of them are on it, making it
To have been left outside, and then to see it – (to have absented oneself).
they're bowing.
there is not breathing – it is not in them
the flow is pouring, over them.
the throat of one pours. The straightened limbs jump up, in the night.
row moving forward, bent – to pour it out.
they follow it – bent –

Woman wading on long yellow grass.
There's the blue sky. She's wading turmoil and some buzzards are on the
grass – that is before her.
Slow low gutting on the long yellow grass.
and the buzzards are on the corpse that is amidst the grass.
hams forward and then back wading – and ahead and behind that in the
grass.
In the blue sky. On the slope. hams extended forward. wading.
on it.
rolled down the grass – and the buzzards on one. Cluster flapping.
that is in the blue sky. Cluster flapping on a corpse.
wading on
indentation in the wave of slopes and buzzards start are on a corpse flapping. up.
hams wading up.
in it.

The buzzards in it had been on the corpses, here and there. Flapping cluster in it on one.

the whirr in that the mixing amidst it in the indentation.

pushed into going into the ocean which is at the edge of this. On the rise, with the others, who're churning. The water is heavy, the rise of it. The living have struggled into it. A shot cracks into it. And a corpse boils. The living churning around it. The lighted sea.

The other feels a crack in her side the hip that is soaking hanging in the heavy water.

blood that comes into the sea from the humans.

And wading in who're shooting they keep on going cracks of shots in it.

churning.

heavy mass.

swimming. the rolls. in the waves.

Having the hip that had hung in the water. In the long grass. Weeds entwined dragging the hip leg lying. Slept deeply before. The men on the mounted pickup truck emerges through grass. A shot in the heavy grass. The leg lying twined in the weed and rolling into indentation.

Buzzards fly up.

from a corpse in the indentation flapping on it.

which is turned over on its trunk.

trunk of woman low wading now.

her on the long grass.

Rolling into indentation of reddish cattle with gentle white faces who're kneeling in it. The kneeling gentle cattle beginning to stand frightened.

The leg is soaked. The kneeling cattle standing, settling. the twined grass. in among them.

Slept in a matted indentation with them.

the men out of the mounted pickup truck overseeing muffled.

Lying by the steer it is not double.

There's a puff. Crack of shots muffled.

Morning comes. it does not come, how can it? the thick slurred cattle kneeling eating in the light air.

the lightened white air. Wheeling oneself forward on a cart, a sled – of the leg. On the sidewalk asking money of the passersby – in it – on the sled.

it is free

for the one they think. for that other who's asking for the money.

on the sled – it is.

a soldier affected by the unburied dead covered with the buzzards in the valleys and not turn that inward.

and then he's in the light air

and not figure out how it unfolds

Wheeling on the sled – having slept in the indentation – deer simply have ticks which become huge until they drop off.

a huge tick in the side of having waded.

they begin singing – soldiers she meets on the road are a choir and they began singing.

into the area of just pulp – only that

One realizing I have to do this myself.

the leg is soaked. She goes on the sled. There's a sandbar out along stretching on which are corpses the buzzards had encrusting flapping. the light air is coming up. no planet. or orb. an orb floating.

Now it's gone.

And out tangled in the yellow grass, on it. The woman wading. There's a corpse in the grass the buzzards sapping it whirling. It's far gone. in the light air.

it can't be that in the long yellow grass

the hams stretch out and running down the slope in the yellow grass. arms twirling flapping being in the grass.

There are weeds. It's dawn. Encounters sensitive man. as in trunk of seal lying on her, rearing – their coming. the light air is coming up. entwined thrashing around. He puts it into her again.

Him rearing, on the trunk
He withdraws it, takes it out
the weeds are still
He puts it back in – on the trunk
Him having gotten an erection
the trunk, the bulb of it in her. after
the dawn

There was this crescent moon hanging with a bright planet in this blue night sky. They were low
in it
the sack of corpse wavered bulb that was created by some behavior
they the orbs weren't held
birds come glancing sucked and then released
by the one or the people in their behavior
it's completely irrelevant

        just the figure of the plant or the plant

drew a figure of a plant, whereas some other traced it and was given the figure to trace and was praised for it – conceived before. Not ability. There is no such. No community exists, and that is not the matter.

Flatness was construed as (was made to be) a barrier put up against the viewer's normal wish to enter a picture and dream, to have it be a space apart from life in which the mind would be free to make its own connections.[1]

have it be life

It isn't. The illness was rampant and took two-thirds of the population and that among the country so there were few laborers. They could ask a high price for their labor, being so few. And so cautioned not to. to do as modesty, is their real circumstance which they should see.

as convention yet
real – as literal

that modesty means something. not struggling. and being free.

Yet the countryside was unworked – who have mind. having been wiped out there by the illness. And those remaining asked cautioned to work at the same low wages as before – when the buds came out on the trees and it was spring.

The budding trees stood out – heartbreaking, to see people starving lying out. how could one be fool enough to have fallen for those who are cruel as being the heart's companion?

love

They fan out as a spray, running – yet there is a huge crowd. The cops are among them, and are before them in a phalanx wearing battle-gear. They lob canisters of teargas into them, which fall. There's the sound of them being thrown. A cloud billows out.

inside in the night the
teargas wafts to people
in a gathering

They break the plate glass windows, the glass coming down in waves, of the banks and the shops. In the day – afterward – the trucks carrying the plate glass come. The only work.

Yet decimated. The crowds break the plate windows again and again.

>   the laborers come – a few
>   working, bringing the plate glass
>   which is roped carried on trucks

Children are playing in the quiet empty yards streets – they come running angry from being chased by a helicopter.

The helicopters patrol, hovering constantly. Chased the children up their own street. Who're made furious.

The people lying starving are the secret – of reality – like the layers of the bud. used to think that and see that is not so.

The (other) is at an Orange Julius stand, having a juice. sitting. She feels ill and is weak, not able to move rapidly or continue on. A cop car stops, and a small crowd gathers around it.

They do something there. Crowded so that she can't see, on the car.

A girl approaches her from there who is thin and dressed raggedly.

She is about fourteen. She wants to hire the (other) to take a package to a house.

She holds it out. It is a small package tied with string. The people around the cop car disperse running, and then before the (other) knows it the girl runs leaving her with it.

>   so they get to joy

not to be given what one wants. And then going to see the animals, is given what one wants simply asking for it – of course one can have that (some thing, in passing). And one can do what one wants. Others didn't know what is meant by this, not having experienced it

>   not experiencing it and
>   having joy
>
>   a man who is
>   so

loving – who is near-by
appeared in a dream
– why?

being given what one wants – it is incredible.

A skinhead approaches her on the street. He is thin frail his head shaved except for a strip of hair in the center, which is long and stands up stiffened. A jagged colored fan. His clothes are ragged. He says he has the address.

The manner in accosting her gentle and sensitive yet lost, as if he might be or imagines *he* would be picking the garbage out from the trash cans to eat, as the others,

and wants desperately
to avoid it

Ahead of her is a crowd of skinheads who're surrounding two boys. Poking at them with their fingers, prodding the chest of a boy. The mood is ugly as if they were going to leap on the two, passersby.

Among them is the boy with the Mohawk whom she'd just met, though he'd run away. His lips are curled in an angry snarl. The boys break away from the group frightened, running.

when –
had
– convention

As she passes, amidst the crowd of skinheads, her glance falls on his arm on which is a tattooed swastika.

If people get any knowledge if it is that that will be valued – as Galileo – later. Whatever dim clouds of blind ignorance that have arisen from despair – we need not despair.

The knees are up jutting almost indistinguishable from the night – running forward.

The man's elbows are on his chest arms cradling a some stick, running and cars move veering of headlights as a car moves to one side or the other slightly swerving in the line the headlights veering. They're in the street.

The black knees are up jutting fast

Then the Mohawk, colored stiff fan on his head, comes up forward and is beside the – knees up jutting, passes it to the former

who goes one hand carrying it running

She returns to her apartment. Hears the man in the next compartment, the shower running, bumping against the compartment.

His windows are all open on the warm night.

The Mohawk boy comes to her apartment building, his face gentle abstracted. The stiff long fan on his shaven head in the light of evening so she's looking out from the doorway blind.

to him

He says the address.

just in the same

She waits for a time, then goes out to her car. An old Valiant which runs and isn't repaired. The car's motor throbs, yet stepping out of it in the dark its tires have been sliced.

which is alive

She walks.

The street in the lighted area is now aswarm with skinheads. There are different gangs, some opposing.

There is no one else there. (except the other) moving through them.

The Mohawk boy is lying to the side in the street. His head is lying on his folded arms, dead, as a child in school.

The (other) kneels by him. The dead body has the swastika tattooed on the arm. It is anonymous.

the boy standing in the light outside her apartment building had no swastika. Having seen his bare arms.

We know we're being shitted when we're four years old and yet we could be going on eighty and still be living in this shitting.

Ads creating a warp. They think that we are in that warp. that isn't ability.

They created this saying this is reality when there is not such. It isn't that. That isn't the center. It isn't.

She delivers the package. The address is a house near Claremont Avenue so when the man comes out afterwards and gets in his car in the dark she begins running. Flags a taxi on Claremont, and tails him speaking to the cabby to the freeway.

She's aware of seeing the Mohawk fan of shaved head, bare arms not of the right, for a moment in the dark by the man's house.

The bay looks like a jewel, and then when they're in San Francisco on Market and the Mercedes pulls over she has the taxi drop her a ways back.

The Mercedes moves again. She runs after in the dark. There's the whirr of the Mohawk fan running behind her.

The stiffened hair fan like a comb going as the legs move—is running in front of her in the dark street.

There's no one around. She's running, the Mercedes stopped parked further on. There was a key in the package. The man has gone to a safety deposit box, the Mercedes whirling in the lamp light turning and moving toward her.

He speeds to her and up onto a curb as she's moving. Pauses as he's hit a pole. There's the sound of the whirring coming from behind.

She turns and sees the Mohawk fan on the head barely turning in the air the legs moving. A whirring sound.

As he's running toward them. The man is cast aside, the bundle he's carrying removed. She's left also, and runs as it's clear night.

(a later section of The Pearl)

Going up to the door and ringing it and saying I was told to say something –
remembering – but I don't know what it is.

Later, selling Fuller brushes and going up to the door. From one house to
another.

And then sitting out on a ridge – a bluff

> that's going
> to be

A valley. And haze wafting up.

Two police went by in their cab wondering if the (other) was all right.

> they feel
> that

The houses seen nestled in the valley – from the ridge – and the clouds at
sunset deep red in a vast carpet coming in. With the ocean outside.

So that the clouds are a plateau covering the town in the valley like heaven.
Now I lay me down to sleep and hope the angels keep me.

At home asleep in her bed.

Sleeping, I was not tired – I lay on the surface – sleeping – not tired –
throughout the night.

There isn't life, that is apparent in the comic book.

A couple come out of their house in their night clothes their car being
blasted bombed blown like a fiery flower crumbling.

They heard the blast, and frightened running outside the car crumbling
unfolding in front of them.

The (other) is lunching across the street – after this had happened that morning and they say that, to her family we sort of laughed who live there next to them.

Down in the town on Shattuck quiet night a car is blown aflame folding.

Laying the brushes out for the housewife – and some that go with the vacuum. Demonstrating brushes, for the hair. Picking up metal balls with the vacuum, when I had the vacuum company job.

And my kid client's up on the roof through the skylight the alarm going and the cops just come in and see him my client having burgled up there.

Just don't do it – we're sitting on a ledge a ridge like a tribe of monkeys – looking down on the valley that is open with gold poppies and purple and blue blossoms so quiet it is outside.

We walked amidst the fields of poppies. that's on the other side. And no one was there.

He doesn't flee or anything. Just crawls up on the skylight.

She's eating in a small Chinese restaurant. He has mind moving – or still – but he doesn't flee.

Face up about fourteen open like a cupcake.

The waving fields with the cups of the gold poppies up and the other blue and purple blossoms with a very blue sky that is behind or in front of them.

It's there, at any rate.

And going down from the ledge the ridge where we'd clung – like monkeys and are in the fields. And a road running up a mountain. There's no potential, though that doesn't matter.

Coming up to the door ringing it and he says he doesn't want any but he'll give me a dollar or how much is it he'll give me that.

So it's forced inward, since outward isn't anything.

A yellow cur mangy abject began following me across town I was in great suffering at the time. Walking all the way through town and up a hill. Cringing when I would turn to it finally and coming on cringing.

Walking on the course meeting a dog which bucked and reared from encountering my eyes. That happened for a period of time. I don't remember why I wrote some thing from that but only that.

The yellow cur cringing and whining hanging back on the hill – winding on the way up to the ridge the bluff.

The (other) is from the lower class and is not in it, and therefore one is a ventriloquist. from Nature.

That isn't anything.

Locked out of the car, she stands a man goes by when she was a child says he has an undercover job shouldn't be spoken to in public. He's walking with another. It is late afternoon. She looks at him he responds. So she asks he says he'll return to open the car. He didn't, she sees him around town.

Out in the heat a shimmering geared as with a cow-catcher or war rig cop car is stopped in the street, for him to go into the little grocery

> or to be not moving there
> in the street

A woman sits elbows on knees out on the steps of her house.

In that heat it's revealed that the boy thin alert who'd retreated up to the skylight and caught there in a wealthy person's house had been found cornered in a warehouse wriggling held by the cop owned by the same person and the cop at the station saying it.

So this will never be seen because it is popular the form of the comic but is it.

As he says it.

At the car wash cleaning the car out several standing black against the puffed blazing clouds. The people, when one is looking into the lighted sky, are black fairly purple in front of the sky.

weeping in it from going home this is complete crap which is real but it's false clouds of mass sky's shining the against and standing several out.

She's in the tearoom of the Biltmore which isn't a café sprawling opening veranda in Santa Barbara and in wicker chairs the colonel who's who and the woman who owns the warehouse who's plump ringed a hairnet on her matted wave trussed wearing a sweater and a fur coat as a wet little muskrat in the heat.

Though not wet, seeming, as she always wore a coat.

At the funeral she rushed up girls! and the mourners couldn't speak to her – wafted heads back in the blow – I wish I had then in this minuteness now to make your acquaintance at first. That can be just in this surface.

Benign with small vicious eyes. The non sequiturs come from the hairnetted wave plump ringed on the crubby fingers trussed in the coat.

The military man isn't a relative is much younger forties fifties was a POW in Vietnam of thirty-four who escaped. She has seen his picture in the newspaper.

So they're in the wicker chairs to speak of a juvenile and there isn't a subject.

In her room, the (other) falls asleep crouched forward – at the end of the bed on her knees. Still, as a horse would sleep standing – little plump hairnetted comes in clawing at her sides get up get up I thought you'd fainted. Having come into her room. Only *they'd* been there.

She'd been reading at the end of her bed.

She goes out on the waves bulk mass of the water but she is holding onto a rope.

Bobbing legs down in the mass, and holding onto a rope pulling to make the way out to a stand that's out bobbing in the shining water. There are people clustered by this platform a stand. In the ocean.

She's exhausted swallowed water.

In bed with others sunburned so that they are. The burned skin brushed by one of the others leg.

The Mohawk boy lying on her – not a skinhead but the hair a strip long stiffened colored fan. He had, running out at night – knees jutting the whirr of the fan slightly (so that'd) been heard behind.

Running down the hill – legs moving fan and then past and ahead in that other place.

Seen before he'd been out in that circumstance.

He lies on her body stretched out and comes thrashing around and the stiff long fan of the head

the fan trembling the body the full length – coming

she has not come and then is afterwards

he is withdrawn and then puts it into her from that – the fan turning and the body and then comes

People are here and there standing in the ocean – a mass on the shore – inflated sports vehicle goes driving on the surface of the water on the inflated large wheels, not amongst them – who're standing to the waist scattered to the sides.

it's out there. being pedalled.

There's a light of the sky on the surface of the water with the people scattered. From that, of their being dispersed.

A few swimming.

Man bending, who's nearer in. the backs of the people in the ocean

A person bending at the shore is conversing with round person. Others two in the foreground standing the backs in the sky.

People walk by.

Take the picture when the feeling occurs, of or from their being dispersed. It isn't there, it's from that.

Lamp beamed on it at night so that the people are here and there in the ocean seen pastey skin

it appeared to be the moon that was the lamp beam – some playing with a ball – on the shown pastey skin of the group in the ocean.

scrutinizing action – as being – the same as the scrutiny

to have just this pulp novel so there is no place to dream.

Photos are not the same as this – as this frame, and so the frame is ahead of what's there. And there's no life

Not concerned about the same dilemmas.

The colonel – demonstrating his cage. in the news and supporting war from within – you have to believe in what in order to – only the view – as that being – fragile.

cleave to that view – he – is (in the news he's died shot ambushed) after he'd been in a bamboo cage trapping animals to supplement his diet of rice and fish in being a POW escaping from there.

within that view of a regime.

and training others for war

The mohawk boy out, trash spilling from the bins on the street – and is the opposite the fan open.

the body stretched out the fan open – coming

the opposite and whirr fan slightly turning running had been which is now lying. After.

She goes out on the waves mass having seen it in the water – crest surge of billows with the black car wading in it sweeping low now in it. Comes up to it. Out in the ocean.

She comes up to it, huge roll of the mass of water – but she comes up to the windows – the car is floating wallowing rolling out sweeping further out.

Peering in to the black car awash – the hairnetted-wave mouth with a rim of blood in it throat cut, trussed in the coat in the front seat. Beside the driver who's slumped facedown on the wheel in the car which is now not there

She's pulling releasing them—at a stuck door, surge of the bulk swell of ocean, and sent out released—before the car wallowing is going to go down—they're buoyant like corks the trussed in the coat sent out from it which is the floating swell.

being within—the boy who the juvenile the client, who'd gotten caught just going up onto the skylight—is now again in trouble. merely attempting to enter the hairnetted-wave mouth's warehouse in which he had formerly been apprehended.

and she's not apprehended—don't speak, trussed in the coat—the water up to her neck released buoyant floating in it out

the swell.

Steal this book.

Go into the warehouse and it is tiers huge long windows high up vaulted and completely empty. It is empty. wonderful.

this is on the radio—reading—happy.

And my kid client who had retreated up on the skylight nimble klutz—if he's going to burgle—and had been in the warehouse, is the opposite—is out on the wharf.

opposite, climbing a crane that are hanging over the yard of wrecked rusting cars, junk—the bank of clouds up in the cranes. or the cranes are in them. the cops are chasing him.

her mouth-rimmed-with-blood, lawyer had ripped her off—not the boy—and is the lawyer for the boy

the opposite in the Mohawk boy lying

when that—nature
is open in it

the Mohawk boy stretched out fan on his head – coming

A bird flies out of her/me of the spirit, is the spirit flying up for a moment, when she is in the yard. So she sees what it is – grief.

Just for an instant so she sees that

And the poor hairnetted-wave mouth with the rim of blood in it, floating out – on the waves swept

Out in the yard, the trains going by on the rails on the highway overpass above and the flowers open unfolding their open and un

painted nails fingernail-polish of in-the-coat drifts out of it

Going out in the water but far out, so the legs hanging while resting or going on in the roll of ocean.

Then wrestling – beside the windows of the black car wallowing swept – not struggling – the hairnet-wave mouth with the rim of blood in-the-coat is in the front seat with slumped driver – and not them as they're dead, or that floating – it's not that, which they are. Or in it. Getting the door open. They float out. Adrift on the hills of waves.

convention – as what's being communicated – and that of possessing a thing. which isn't so – nor is there being communicating.

Not seeing this or remembering as it is real. Their drifting out of the car and out onto the ocean.

> this doesn't come from within –
> it really comes from
> experience

> > walking in sunlight – as
> > experience and
> > the birds chortling in the middle

> not seeing this and
> completely free

> > seeing that – experience
> > and is so

1. T. J. Clark, *The Painting of Modern Life*.

Orion

Essay on the comic book

Not having friends because of not being that. There aren't any.

The conception of this does not exist for those who are from the highly organized civilization which is based in the view that being free is having consumer goods.

Not using the mind.

We see as in this – the comic book – one frame at a time.

only not in
the comic book

This other civilization, which they are viewing (who are from the highly organized civilization), does not have order. There is no order. A bus driver is a function, who might drive until running out of gas. Not knowing where he is going, and seemingly not even wondering. It is not a matter of where the bus is to be going. Not merely from not being organized. Though it is repressive.

Consuming is not the ideal.

The repression emanates from the state but the refusal of order is rebellion.

Not using the mind is rebellion – at first – in the comic book.

Went to the arcade

but only alone

that is the department store. It was a city which had a high glass-domed ceiling, tiers, hundreds of compartments with only a few goods, interior bridges.

The crowd pressing into the cells. A crowd waiting in line outside one cell.

The (other) is beside herself. In where the mother whales are suckling the babies, stillness, the foam spray of the turmoil being on the outside. She is right up next to them, amongst them.

The side of one of the creatures.

> mind isn't in
> this

In the hive of the arcade, the intruder foreigner has come in surrounded by a mob – who're the mirror images, the reverse of the civilization and don't move.

> mind is before
> it

standing amongst them who're standing eating and don't move yet bump her –

> it is outside
> them, the crowd
> of the arcade department
> store

The crowd seeming to jeer at us leaving in droves having it was found later seen banners advertising it as a strip show. Not knowing at the time. And so the young man having been jeered compared it to after coming out, discovered by his classmates, being ridiculed on the schoolbus.

Those of the highly organized – ordered – civilization ridiculing for using the mind

> I'd written a paper which the teacher
> read to us and my friend ridiculing me
> after as being a vegetable

I did not speak to this friend again.

                    and hurting the
                    crowd

The effect of the comic book unintentionally is hurting the crowd

            hurting the crowd
                                    from that
                                    them

from themselves – I had written a paper and the teacher read it to the class
so the friend afterwards screaming that I was a vegetable ridiculing using the
mind.

                    floating as themselves
                                    on itself

The system there was completely different from the individual, from the
people.
    who were at the same time the reverse image of the ordered civilization

            experience
            as learned
                                    experience is learned
                                    from them

Those who are without social power are less inclined to see reality as orderly

                    not from their view

less inclined to see the social construction as unified

                    is the reverse

Being in the crowd and don't move is the reverse image and so neither joy
or use of the mind in them.

                    before it
                                    changing them
                                    from inside

and so only in rare instances is the comic book in rapport with the experience of its readers.

the emancipation from experiences

The people who are going to work walking with their briefcases or with shopping bags past the sea on the sand – on their way – the moon in the sky above them.

Our collective sense of not making connections which is seeing as fragmentary series is not a given.

Essay on the comic book

(Walter Benjamin's *Charles Baudelaire: A Lyric Poet in the Era of High Capitalism*, Verso Press)

The crowd – is not conformity.

The people from the highly organized civilization – coming to the other civilization which had no order, though repressed – were hungry ghosts.

they had thin, narrow throats and huge bellies so that it had to be beforehand, others had to open to them

to get the narrow throats open so that they could eat and be released

communing occurs as
we have created it and
choose it

the hungry ghosts do not see communing

people do not feel there to be a rapport with the comic book of the Metropolis for their experience has changed

it has occurred before

it is the exact same thing as experience

so a meanness emanated from the thin-throated people unable to eat who had huge bellies – in the civilization of the bus driver who drives as a function without knowing where he's going, which is without order as being rebelling

                    and creating
                    imperialism, from the two civilizations

Experience is a matter of tradition, in collective existence as well as private life. Serial as the assembly line.

the comic book is the exact same thing as experience – before it

                              only

to enable the hungry ghosts to get their throats open to eat – which were reversed in to the civilization in which no taxis could be flagged, or they wouldn't take the person who'd stopped them if they didn't feel like it.

The metros in the repressed civilization go deep many floors down into the ground.

                         heads bowed
                         filing

they all said there is no light in their eyes – said by the narrow-throated hungry ghosts with huge bellies who were protruded as funnels into the Metropolis.

One of these who'd come there, pale with the liquid blood interior seen in the mouth – went on the escalator that ran into the deep metro. The same as in its own ordered civilization, the corpse of a bum lay.

           now they are being excluded from the stations
           to live, unless they have a ticket

to be emancipated from experiences, in the comic book – to be it as such.

                 to have no other self
                 than in the comic book[11]

and so for one not to be in rapport with it – or with experience – as being Baudelaire's discovery.

being outside of the experiences of the civilization – that can be by these not having order

The man driving a car in the (his) metropolis which before setting out is

11. You tell it to someone when they can't see it and it's invisible to them.

going to run out of gas, and looking driving in narrow mired dark alleys for a filling spot – not knowing if one will be there – smoke stacks pouring clouds into the night sky.

That Baudelaire felt the above as suffering – not being able to have historical experience – making that discovery but it surfaced as suffering.

in the person contemplating

There not being historical experience – is the comic book.

The narrow-necked from the ordered civilization have no experiences.

in them
afterwards

Expecting such of friendship, in them, as being convention – which is not convention.

the comic book – is calm.

The Geographical History of America reads like seeing it on the retina. It is light. dying. subjection to gang ridiculing.

Essay on the comic book

(Each of the lines or paragraphs is one of the frames of the comic book.)

The crowd marks the split between themselves and experience.

They construct all the buildings to be the same.

That's a different way of regarding; so the man whose function it is to drive the bus doesn't know where he's going or seem to wonder.

> as it is before
> him

Not using the mind – which then occurs in the frames of the comic book afterward – with the bus driver from the civilization without order though it is repressed

> then

I was out in the cornfields, and sky – and people would pull alongside shouting obscenities saying to go back where one'd come from.

What is the relation of action – someone's – to the unfolding of phenomena?

The farm boys coming up alongside with obscenities out in the fields.

Wavering alongside and if one says they're from there, their exploding feeling insulted.

Which is really funny.

Just say back to them they're from there and they erupt.

At a streetlight, out in the fields – out in nowhere – and they waver there alongside shouting.

then feel hurt in public

from what had been before.

One cannot expect to be a bum.

The reverse of that – which is before

where people used to lie in the train stations

and now they have to have a ticket

Not using the mind – is contemplating – in the comic book.

The newspapers have created the impression of disjointed experiences. But I don't read them.

anyway, we're not in these experiences
is the impression created by the newspapers which
do not allow us to make connections

Not having historical experience – is the comic book as the form of the serial novel. Though popularly we're supposed to be in them – this is a deprivation created by the newspapers themselves.

The moon is in the day sky, now out in the cornfields – rather than in the civilization which does not have order, though it is repressed.

The farm boys hanging wavering floating at the crossroad – alongside, shouting obscenities.

are from the ordered civilization where the bum lying has died in the subway station.

as such they're not in experiences – as the reverse image of the deprivation created by the newspapers.

The serial – but then being before it

And afterwards there's only that
They are out by the fields
These boys were shouting, maybe because they're together – wavering
hanging leaning out coming alongside.
I feel depressed – I'm tired of being made fun of.
Farm boys who're just youths floating leaning out
People standing like the cattle in the sea – waist deep, standing

on grass

being invalidated and nothing
is the reverse image of the ordered civilization
and one is calm

I was in a huge crowd which was a sea of people at a rally in a square.

standing

Claustrophobia of feeling that one was going to throw up – in the
crowd – and moving through the crowd.

then

who don't move, though there was one woman elbowing moving
through the crowd propelled. Her swimming through them, I moved in the
opening following her.
Someone else saying – outside, on the outskirts – that they had had a
feeling of going to throw up in the crowd. They were outside then. It not moving.
My feeling of going to throw up in it and the woman swimming elbowing
as the only moving being

flags banners held up on the mass

And if you took pictures they turned stolidly, staring thinking you were
taking pictures of them. that that would be repressive

standing.

I woke up tying my shoe fully dressed, which I'd done myself, crying. From this, I perceived there was no one there. Saying this to a friend when I was an adult, he said: that concern is such to you that the episode occurred. which itself might not happen to someone else. something else would happen to them.

sort of like finding your way out of a paper bag.

Man who is a soldier – in an invaded country. His army has brutalized and killed people there in the countryside. Their dead wouldn't be allowed to be seen or presented in his own land.

So the expression of this is he comes upon only the corpses in their countryside of his own people.

          and will never go back[1]
          to his own civilization

              the jewel

is not doing so.

This was as close as they could come.

          on the part of what had been the conquered people
          and are not that they appear as only calm

A man riding in a taxi, the taxi driver has a conversation about being in the war. He seems very aggressive.

The one thing about being there was he enjoyed killing and can't do that here.

having someone them at the point of his gun and then killing them made him feel –

          the comic book – using the mind one
          can't do here either

1. *The Geographical History of America* has chapters because it is calm.

It was not acceptable to criticize oneself.

The (other) is in her apartment. At night happy the man in the neighboring compartment on the other side of the wall bumping against the wall — reading. Him urinating, in his stall.

The night is so still — outside — reading.

Walking back at night.

The branches of the trees hanging, she walks through them.

A mutt comes running out. It jumps in the air — as it's little — and bites a tuft of the artificial fur of her jacket. Tears off a bite. It has done this before.

Mutt.

A man steps out of the trees. Innocent, wounded, he is someone who emits poison as would a scorpion with the tail raised over the back — before — and injecting the poison out of the bulb of it.

He is innocent. He wants her to do a job. Find his daughter, yet his manner is skittish in the sense of tough and wounded.

She returns to the apartment. The man of the adjoining compartment, who'd urinated in his stall. stamping.

He does not want to be seen — the poison bulb tail wounded before

He is not like the soldier who'd been given a seat in a boat — who'd disguised as a Buddhist monk —

realistically this is because the passenger in it is a monk but subliminally those who'd been the ones invaded are completely calm.

> so he can
> not go to his own civilization

can be allowed not to.

but the poison bulb wounded is not contemplative like this.

> he seems to be

why?

She is talking to him out on the street — in the day.

wangling like sending a hook out

His daughter had apparently blended into the street life and he hadn't seen her for a year or sought for her – before.

Aged landlady – this was before it came apart, and she died – needing her, very old drunken blissful seen staggering in the yard in the plants.

Happening into her there. Where she'd seem to come out.

Baudelaire's discovery of not being in experience

in the crowd

She sees the man's daughter on the street one day – the (other) is with him who can therefore see her.

The girl coming up in the stream, the three go into a coffee shop. Bulb wounded poison emitting that into her, the girl looks at him with a simple open sympathy.

She says that she loves him. A disapproval emanating from him, bulb wounded innocent intimates afterward to the (other) that the job has not yet been completed.

The comic book – being written as there is a market for it.

inventing the sense of a private psyche – which had been before – is an expression of the split between self and experiences.

and is aware that it is that.

so it had not existed – doesn't after this.

Man acted for our CIA for/in the other's war and isn't tried.

Isn't tried since the proof is classified by our CIA for whom he works. Our utterly corrupt system.

The man is released. She goes to see him and a man in the street is lying dead beaten covered in blood and being washed by the rain. The rain is pounding slanting in sheets on the street. the man is being washed for his grave. Her having come to the man's door, a small group in streetlight is hovering around the mound lying there. Shred.

A patrol car is parked but dimmed in the rain.

Thin blood running off the mound. Remnant or rim of blood on it tuft – film on it.

yet not being in one's own civilization

the jewel

she thinks.

And continues in the rain to his place which is an apartment building, dark in approach lighted in the vestibule.

He won't talk to her. He's lying on the bed, mumbling to himself. A bottle of whiskey is on the bureau. Thin indistinct face with the lack of features of a mole

no features of the face – doesn't answer her. She sets the bottle down.

Mumbling to himself face up lying on the bed.

She sips, burning sensation in the pit within her. Sets the bottle down. The neon sign from across the street is dim on him – though she's turned on a switch. He doesn't answer her.

gurgling – of him. With no features on the face.

working at this too hard so that the burning sensation of the whiskey in her is burnt out – before, when it gets there it's empty. It's relaxed. There is no cauterized. The jewel. What follows it is muffled and empty.

She's out on the street in the rain.

She's in the hotel room sick. The hotels are drab wings blocks-long so that one cannot get to the main door from a wing. One has to refind the central shaft by walking along dark halls.

She could have died like a rat in the room. They wouldn't have sought her. No friendship or how does that occur in others. The buildings constructed to duplicate before.

She puts the bottle down again. Relaxed.

No more of this thick food covered in fat.

———————

She hasn't been eating, feels light-headed free. It's extremely cold.

freezing, steam comes off of the immense palladium swimming pool – the swimmers arms on it.

163

the arms dipping.

their elbows – wings – on the immense swimming pool. Rungs of the arms rake across it.

Mole no features on the face batted buffeted in the rakes of arms lifted again and again on the swimming pool.

Steam arising from the palladium

no features on the face buffeted flaccid caught in the rakes of arms crossing the pool.

Beside the dead mole featureless face up, is the girl – amidst the mass of swimmers.

Resting side by side with him – adjoining.

Mole face up.

She stirs.

The girl's face becomes alert yet is in the mechanism of the rake of arms doing a lap on the pool.

The (other) is held up and blurred – seeing the girl swaying beside the mole, but gradually recovers. There's a motion on the sideline.

A jet or blur darts to the stairs of the raised outdoor swimming pool and goes down to the street.

It's freezing.

The (other) recoils, gradually recovering and then begins to run.

She ran after the figure – which had gone.

Goes down the street.

The figure had gone into the metro to the deep stairs of escalators, rungs of them.

leading deep underground, the deep bronze escalators descend to where she comes to him still on it – pursed white face puckered of very old woman, turned upwards, whom she passes blurs.

Coming to him, hitting her in the gut.

Is sent backward falling down the escalator. with her running toward him.

He lies crumpled at the bottom, and a deep stain spreads on the front of his chest.

The assassin of the mole featureless face up is shot – and dying, says nothing to the (other).

To say nothing – the bulb tail injected calls her up the next day, injecting as if onto a gel (she's in her apartment). She wonders what the poison wounded innocent wants as surveillance of his daughter.

He seems helpless. He'd been a marine.

The girl had been left. He's complaining and yet holding back.

She recognizes it as a feeler.

The dart a ball, hitting her in the gut – floats backwards out in the air shot and crumpled at the foot of the stairs.

the curled ball, having whirled, diving for her – punching her in the gut. His back hurls forward.

The dark curved steep moving stairs – a hump, goes down slowly like a falls. to meet him.

She lies in her apartment.

Billows of dark exhaust pour out of some near-by trucks. And sweeps into their faces, it's night. They jump out of the trucks. Asked to unload and load the heavy stacks in the cold. Men are running.

Her just descending slowly on the falls to meet him. Just as a ball was hanging in the air batted by two people on the beach. The ball was in the black sky as she's facing the sun – it's in the light.

(The ball was black because it was in the sky – as the people were batting it on the beach – and it was in the bright light.

it wasn't moving.

She darts back up the metro stairs – that are going down. And runs; a man is running.

It's freezing.

They're in the arcade glassed-domed with a mass of people crawling. He's not running so she can't see him.)

Standing in line, with the mass still – she reaches the counter of the shop and then is elbowed out by the person directly behind.

She's outside the line. No one is moving.

Stands in it again – no shoving and when she's reached the counter again, elbowed out by the next person behind. very still, no moving.

(except when being elbowed out by the one person as she's about to reach the front.)

she goes on. Enters a café, the people standing no sound from their chest, a din but not arising from them being mute. She is beside them. There are counters where they stand. One person'll bump her when she reaches a counter like a berth.

She stands out in the center and is bumped from a spot she'd take. again. calm. no faces are turned. (to each other or her.)

She can't see him.

The gel receives the injection – the entire mob, hurting the crowd. The bulb tail wounded before – he doesn't associate with them. The city is laid out, drab

Preaching to some people one imagines to be the herd – out there.

They are not in this – not doing that.

She can barely recognize the carved flutes on the corners of buildings because her eyes can't see them.

The cops had checked over the assassin of the mole featureless face

as if for lice

and the man who shot him getting away in the crowd.

The perversion of the consumers. distortion of their complaints. (not those of the unmoving mass.)

as if for lice shred.

being in the unmoving mass

The aged landlady blissful bonkers – with craft, and yet not needing her care then – like a bark (boat) amidst the plants – she needs her and it's come apart. she thinks.

the jewel
It's not being in the other civilization
but rather not in her own

which is visible. very old woman comes out of drug store and gets in taxi; she'd been at the soda fountain counter. The (other) comes up to ask her something, and the cab driver is helping her in the cab.

doesn't want to be in it anyway or
the other

They having the red carpet rolled out to make them be that which is convention itself. He has that and is not it. I came to town and those who were convention itself didn't speak to him – they didn't want me to. Driving in the car coming in, I saw him standing. The man driving afraid of his shining ability feared meeting him. I wanted to call him later, in order not to bother him then. We went on. When I said this later to others outside there they create convention itself. They interpret my action of seeing him and being in it as not objective which is theirs. They say my being in it changing it. They are the same as them. He is the same as myself.

the elderly frail face frayed – without features, not having money but having been at the fountain eating a sandwich.

white-haired tend to gather at the soda fountain and to take taxis back.

the (other) goes up inviting herself into the cab. She recognizes the extremely old woman though bearing no resemblance to any others and she's happy to see her.

who's open.

the frayed is weak and she lies back in the cab. People are walking on the street, neither the unmoving mass or the distortion of shoppers. It's a clear, light day.

They see a man on the street, to whom the frayed beckons. He gets into the back seat.

Thin his entire frame has no features. He talks to her the elderly condescendingly – assuming things they know; he works in an office somewhere. He says the value of something is in whether it can be sold.

Duh.

The elderly doesn't regard him as unusual.

We've made people simply separate from each other – though the frayed's not that. And so the (other) is intensely lonely and the elderly one is not.

He says things.

She feels beaten. In the clear, light day.

Feeling incredibly tired – sleeping in her apartment. She's in the sleep deeply. The next day it's clear and light.

Cauterized, where there's something empty and clear after that. She begins to weep.

There isn't anything there to be weeping about.

(Having been out on the street flagging cabs which wouldn't stop – wanting to cry. Once. It follows that one can cry and no one will care, and this is a great relief. So she stood and wept. the jewel.)

then found a cab.

The man on the street of the frayed's cab, is that one's grandson making him the brother of the girl.

Going into the metro.

the marine's – injecting out onto gel – there far back on the moving stairs. The (other) sees the head of the consumer man from the cab down flowing to meet him. A person slumps on the moving stairs.

Shot, but there isn't any sound in the metro.

The girl is beside the corpse.

the frame moving forward of the girl

The (other) is running.

Yet the consumer man from the cab falls forward. and on the runner —
who has passed him on the escalator.

He falls on her so that she goes down yet he's dead.

The marine is helpless.

Some person has been shot who was near the girl.

That's what they say to the cops.

And the dead man — unlike the unmoving mass, had been amidst them,
when she'd been in the café looking for him.

Their not moving in the arcade café, and her parting them.

His money's dependent in the mole featureless' dealings in other coun-
tries. Embedded in it. He'd been shooting the girl while the (other)'s running
to her — for she's aware of this.

The marine's helpless — and shoots him.

She's failed — there isn't a relation between action and this; not cauterized,
clear after it.

She lies in her apartment.

   one is taught   when a
child which is immediately unbelievable to that child

> At a time when many people were dying, I saw this
> tiny tot running across the floor in an airport.
> A little creature that had cropped up. And I thought
> What's the point? it's just going to die.

the civilization with order having created the clear series of events.

to be a comic book form. It invalidates itself.

It will use itself up as pulp and be regarded as nothing. It is not 'discursive,'
'analytical' 'method' — by in some ways reproducing such and not being
that.

If the series is inhibited, cauterized early-on no relations occur between
people.

one can't expect to be a bum — according to them.

it's invisible to them who don't see it
because they interpret experiences in reverse
as not valued – or non-existent
then depart from them

that the marine helpless had killed his own son.

The (other) is receiving as if onto a template the mean lack of considera-
tion as of gang ridiculing from a woman in a group; they're seated in a coffee
shop.

as they are friends – and so one has to be inhibited

Excusing herself, she goes out. Outside, the street is quiet.

Having only a moderate living – not using the mind – is contemplating

She begins to weep, and this is such a relief.

She looks up and can see the stars.

There is Orion. Orion is lying on his side, falling into the Southern Hemi-
sphere.

In the day, the white-haireds gather at the drugstore at the soda fountain
counter, then take taxis back.

People walk on the street.

A white-haired comes out, and goes by taxi back

---

simply representational and serial – is contemplating

Comic book 2

We're having the view that experience itself is convention. as a sense we've
created.

making it and so relieved

Working at the soda fountain, days of serving sandwiches at the counter.
I heard that a young woman had robbed the bank which is a block away get-

ting away coming up the street. The dye they'd put in the bag went off and stained her.

She was caught by a cop.

To see experience itself as only convention is necessary to them.

Coming up the street a few days later it's a clear light day and yet a hungry ghost the thin neck unable to take in is in front of a person.[15]

There are shops.

the meanness was like a light that was shined back through us. from having a sense of being that is gregarious.

> feeding in as
> calm throughout but
> not inside
> or inside too

and so friends are being passive supportive. not themselves.[2]

People walk by.

She goes to meet the girl in jail.

She feels depressed and the girl is alert as if a cork that is floating wanting her brother to be located and to be notified of her being in jail.

The (other) is quieted, going out in the large, cool hallways of the justice building where the girl is interned.

She comes around a corner in it. There's a crowd in the hall.

A boy who's on the edge of the crowd outside, comes up to her.

He says he's the girl's brother.

The (other) feels very tired and goes down in the street. Overwhelmed, blurred by weariness, she lies down. Garbage from a bin is strewn, the alley's wet yet she's unable to move. She's slept three nights on the street.

When it's morning, it's cold.

The street is empty.

15. Conventional is a joyless life – that which is experience.[16]
16. Define that person who's rebelling as alienated in order to make them invisible.
2. (The comic book is calm because it is serial.)

There is a grey and pink thin light. Grey line and pink line with the thin light in between in the sky in front of her.

———————

The (other) feels utterly beat. She's seated at a counter in a coffee shop early. The eggs are in film lying there. The coffee is acid in her yet thin as water.

Her waitress refills her cup.

She's on the stool in the light.

The boy, who's the brother, comes in coming to her. She isn't feeling very forthcoming.

Besides he doesn't say what it is

She stares down at the food. He has a desperate motion, wearing ragged clothes.

Afterwards she accompanies him to his family business. It is a metal shop, an old foundry. Defunct. Amid the rows of tables on which are trunks of metal – the trunks have openings – is a corpse. It is weeks old.

The boy is not anywhere, having led her

The cops swarm down on the place, mad at her. and want to know where he is when the girl has gotten out of jail earlier in the day on bail.

The moldered corpse lying there shred and she's sitting hearing them.

She's seated smelling the stench of the flowering bum – they say.

Where'd the girl get the bail? Their family is nonexistent now and so is their family business.

She's wondering why they're so interested. She's at home lying in bed, the man stamping in the compartment next door.

It's a warm night.

falls asleep – so that it's pushed into the day. Empty. out strolling on the street.

A man who is a construction worker is out and is reversed. And so he comes.

Coming very strong. Inactive.

She's walking toward him on the street.

It's clear, empty street.

She's very happy. The man coming out

The corpse of the foundry was not a bum, or was as it's the same.

It's the same

She's out and by shops a hungry ghost unable to get the neck open – funnel, stands in front of her as she passes.

She walks up the street.

by him.

the jewel

having known real samurai warrior
but when she was a small child
who's recognized

now it floats away from her.

the gang ridicule and condescension of the people in the group seated at the table who're friends has made her inhibited.

seeing the man who's the brother recognizing
the young samurai of whom
she has a picture

and who's floated away from her, freeing her – having known him when she was a small child.

he comes strongly out in the
clear empty street

The endless stream of rebuke as of gangs which they friends and strangers would do to anyone. They do to anyone. Yet it has inhibited her.

The girl has jumped bail.

She's in the arcade department store, the glass-domed ceiling over bridges with the unmoving mass crawling on them.

the people are in lines leading in to the compartments and so still.

She sees the girl's brother as he is running.

He has been injected ahead of the stream.

And in the rear embedded in the crowd is a faint movement of men who are running after him. They are retarded in it.

He is in a clearing.

She is helpless beginning to run to him.

Shots come out of the crowd from the men chasing hurting the crowd.

She's helpless running to him.

The boy falls

The men are retarded in the movement in the mass.

When she gets there, the boy has gotten up and gone. A splash of blood.

She's in the businessman's clean, empty office. He is polite. He rings for his secretary who brings in a file of the formerly attached family business.

but which has now been vacated – he says.

the papers indicate the business has been subsumed by the other company.

the bum flowering corpse had been murdered – was a partner in the former business.

the cops a few were in on this, on the take

Not caring, for the origin of the flowering corpse thus.

This man's arrested

then

She goes back to her apartment through the boughs up the street.

Comic book 3

The people are trying to perceive them through their actions.

or perceive their actions through them.

She has been doing nothing. lying in her apartment. A man comes wanting her to do a job. He's pissy a friend. She knows he's badmouthed her to cops – and so he's having her do some job?

contemplating – is in him.

wants her to check on someone who's buying his house. in run-down neighborhood.

they've apparently skipped before.

so she goes there, where the main work is junk. a junk yard – people pushing shopping carts on the street to it filled with rubbish.

maybe junk also.

people standing

Birds fly up off a tree.

The buyer has moved in. He isn't speaking, lying on the bed. nothing forms. He's awake.

The door is open letting in a clear light. trash is on the floor inside.

She leaves and goes to get something to eat.

Eating out on the walk a streak of rose in the sky.

She goes back and the man has died.

She says that to the cops.

He's been throttled with a cord around his neck. There isn't anything taken from the place apparently in which there wasn't anything to take.

The pissy man is ridiculing, condescending and yet she is just of ordinary people, not the unmoving mass or the shallow consumers.

who're the jewel

if she could return to them.

the corpse has been dead since she was there – starting then.

She says to her client, he won't skip – that's funny

then it's inside

She pulls away with him complaining in the car

if she turns left he'll have a fit. she thinks.

In fact, he insists on getting out of the car having a fit stamping. He's not going to pay her.

She's in the vegetable market, picking out vegetables. Two men go after the checker. heavy-set barrel coming for him.

just seeing it on the retina

He runs and she sees it is the girl's brother.

He's injected as if slowly outside the stream that surrounds and is in the market and shops.

People coming to the market in the evening

as if fish roe in a slick on the light ocean, a line of sand below it. The light waves coming down.

The male fish on it – on the slick.

He injects outside of the gel. running.

She's calm.

This is something else, outside.

She goes to her client's office which is a mess and has his secretary let her see his balance.

It turns out they who're gambling thugs were going to foreclose on piss' house. and they murder the corpse thinking it was him. And he knows it.

He knew it then. and had taken off.

She's going to her apartment.

Coming back up the street, she runs through the boughs.

then having been injected out into the warm night.

Fireflies other calm insects.

it's trash. She's been doing nothing and her life is nothing – and so invalidated is calm.

not from it

not from being invalidated.

they've done nothing, the people at the market – are doing nothing

regardless of ridiculing
gang subjection and they are

aren't in a state – which is before in the series

she's not of ordinary people when
they're aren't

We've attacked and apparently routed the government of a country and
are saying it is freedom for them. perverting it – and the newsmen are – creating a series of delusions.

the line and the other line
and the light in it

Being invalidated – is calm

the jewel

from what? So is this.

which is emancipated from experience anyway

The men – on the slick. of the crowd. The light waves coming down.

———————

This is invalidated.
We've invaded a country saying they're brutalizing our people in their
country. Imperialist civilizations can brutalize freely. They're helpless.
The light waves coming down.
This is simply trash.
A man comes up to her on the street. This is reversed. It's the pissy man
whom she hasn't seen since he'd taken off leaving the corpse in the house he's
trying to sell. The corpse had been throttled by gambling thugs who think it's
him.
He has moved back into his house again, after the corpse had been carried
from it. There is still trash on the floor inside.

trash on the floor of his car as well

he'd never been away. she thinks.
it breaks down as it is emancipated from experiences but in reverse.
the girl's brother floating running on the roe of the crowd

not only that has not occurred but
is in between

as is the imperialism, invading the small country. creating delusions. their being helpless.

and the boy running. he's in the crowd. outside of them with the men following him.

then it's there in
him out of the roe. which is the crowd.

they're the murderers of the junk freak in the guy's house and are aware of her having seen them. (she did not see them.) they're running

coming toward *her*. there's the whirr of a broom handle which sticks in the one guy.

raised arm of the boy. he's moving

running his hams stretched out in the crowd surrounding the market in the evening

———————

applying for a job in a casino, she wasn't hired because she was living unwed with a man.

we have the sense that experience itself is convention. I don't.

bird flapped by her slowly on rust-colored long grass in the pale sky.

almost brushing

episodes are in the newspapers as to seem the same as experiences.

And the comic book in being serial is this.

They blew up the casino boss in his car, in the lot of the casino where she worked. not the one where she hadn't been hired. muscular man blown who was honest.

That was experience and so we are emancipated from it—she is doing nothing, and her life is nothing.

She is picking out vegetables in the market. People coming to the market in the evening.

what is being said with someone there is that there is no content in a conversation except coming to the market in the evening. we have a sense there is not interiority, which is being nothing.

there's struggling in her.

tired going out and lying down in the street. she's unable to move. she can't get back. she sleeps there. lying huddled on the street.

then there's no struggling.

there is no relation between there not being interiority and the flowering corpse.

we have a sense of duration. no we don't.

there is no relation between the flowering corpse and the child

there's struggling

no struggling between the flowering corpse and the child. who's later.

she's doing nothing

She's sitting in the coffee shop in the morning. The man comes in who'd hurled the broom handle stuck in the man running toward her. Had seen her there before. He's aware and doing nothing.

only separate from people in convention

this is seeing this as of negatively which is
the same from being inside

and so it's really knowing we're free already
in front of it — (that we're in front of it)

he wants to hire her to find a man who's holding the papers to his family's subsumed business.

and he'd led her in to finding the flowering corpse — leaving her with it.

there's no relation between a sense of duration and the child and there's a relation between that and Baudelaire's experience.

he wants the papers to get it back. the family having died in a fire. arson he thinks.

it is necessary to them that experience itself be convention. then there is not meaning to it. that is fine. the jewel.

She's in the neighborhood where the living is junk.

Coming down the street. trash on it.

She rings at the address given her. If he has the address why doesn't he go, and yet wanting to be peaceful and have someone else handle this. That's the way he represented it to her.

No one comes. She goes around back. There is an old woman lying in a chair. dyed hair. She is a dull metallic rose-colored bat. speaks that way. giving the information of the whereabouts of her husband. lying there a sack.

driving there's a green old chevrolet

gets to the warehouse and walks in

there's a dark shade area.

he's back in there. heavy-set rolled sitting back. with the barrel of a shotgun resting in his middle.

There's a flash from him. firing and another flash and he rolls out. dead from the man behind her.

— she's been dumb. he speaks to her calmly. she's being asked by the cops. later.

going through the bough of trees. as if being a man repairing shoes. the man urinating in his stall — is calm

we have a sense of that. the people coming to the market in the evening.

dovetailing with Baudelaire's experience

the man goes out lying down in the street. by some buildings. it's wet and cold. he can't move from being tired.

In the morning it's clear.

Just seeing it on the retina.

So they meet. we are tradition – that of Baudelaire being outside of experiences. no we're not.

not going anywhere

it appears the same as experience – and is not

The man goes out sleeping under a bridge with a stream, cars streaming over the bridge and the light in the center of the clouds.

The cars moving into the light – are just seen on his retina.

There are huge birdsnests in the trees jutting out that have been built by people – bums

the nests are here and there on the plain that is beneath the bridge in the light.

The child has no sense of the flowering bum.[14]

the event does not take place until it is experienced – in the comic book it is afterwards, so we are not in experiences.

we have a sense of a dialectic in history. that is not there. the comic book is seeing on the retina.

14. then suffering isn't anything as it's oneself.

Chapter 2

The dull metallic dye of hair rose-colored bat as if she is a sack covered with peach fuzz-down is mourning at the grave site. tears coming out. the old woman's face is distorted and tears on it.

sack who's emptily weeping at the grave.

It's morning, the grave is open still after the ceremony – a few dumpy relatives out on the lawn.

a fake covering of plastic green grass was draped over the mound of dirt so as not to see the dirt.

down on the sack distortedly weeping. teeth in her mouth. tears coming out. which rack her.

the lawn stretches around, a limousine slowly coming through the narrow road.

The (other) is asked before the ceremony by the depleted widow to protect her – which startles her as not having meaning and she herself figuring in the death of the old woman's husband.

grief-stricken old woman. The (other) feels uncertain.

Sitting in her office, with the light coming through the slats of the blinds into the room, she isn't considering or having any materializing feeling.

One is interested in someone because she's married to someone, who is wealthy. not for herself. and one knows this about oneself and doesn't care.

The (other) does not care in seeing this – so there is no interiority.

she isn't interested in the hungry ghosts

the jewel

sitting there is in her.

Sitting in the coffee shop, the people are seated around the counter. a fly is on the lighted window.

the birdsnests made by people in the jutting trees are on the plain underneath the bridge of streaming cars.

there's a field out there in which wild swans winter sitting as a flock on it.

The (other) goes to the man's, of the broom handle stuck in the man, foundry. of the flowering corpse. she's not going to wait.

It's quiet. the corroded metal – trunks with multiple openings through which would be strung cables, for ships – is lying on rows of tables.

There's a long window with shafts of light.

so they meet. the light.

Coming to the neighborhood where the living is junk, she goes around back. The old woman is lying in the chair stretched out. fear for her.

Yet she's snoring, down on her, and wakes squinting remembering pain. tears coming from her. screwed up face and streaking. sack lying in the chair giving the information.

The jutting trees on the plains in which are birdsnests made by people out – bums sleeping in them.

The young woman goes down to the dock yard. The ships are coming in. a mass of water with the light on it from clouds.

Men are unloading a ship. people in the category of families. that's crap, they're not families. out on a plain. smoke coming up. off the plain. just crowds streaming away.

she's telling her all she knows

the information is only that the freight has something to do with the foundry. and yet the downy woman in the light hasn't ever seen any freight in there.

The (other) sees a man because he had been in the metro station. She's standing out on the dock and so there is nothing to lose.

on the flat plate of the truck – the empty flatbeds attached to the cab.

the cab's moving – rolled on lightly crouching on the shaking plate.

no sides – the shaking flat plates – to the cab

rearing shaking running on the shimmying flat

lightly crouched running – jumped onto the attachment that's ahead.

the cab hauling ass on the road. goes around a curve. flat-beds thrown swaying. she stands thrown balancing swaying on flat.

rolls lightly crouched. regains her balance. the cab tears into the road dust coming from the wake.

orbs shining in the night – the vast array

lightly running – she's to reach the cab, switchback it's swaying with him flooring the gas.

high sea blue sparkling on the mountain road – and throws her. rolling crouching. the flats swaying.

she manages to get into the straps that hang under the truck. held in them as in boughs. high blue brilliant sea is by her.

deep blue sea goes by flatbed

the hawks and flocks of sparrows are even with her

the cab and its attachment barreling along so that he believes she has been thrown.

The (other) steps down. It is night. It's quiet. the truck has come to a rest. hanging boughs. the men are in a coffee shop.

the men in the coffee shop in the light are CIA. that means they will wipe her out. they will rub out the dull metallic rose-colored old woman. who is weeping. fragile sack as is the detective.

whatever the dealings with the driver of the cab-flatbeds swaying – who will not be arrested.

the package like a white cocoon is tied to the bottom of the truck. as she had been. resting side by side with her. she loosens it, cocaine, and takes off with it.

running, with it under her arm. this is dying, but it is dying anyway.

She can hear voices behind her. in the dark starry night.

the man, raised arm throwing broom handle, had not known.

warm hands.

speaking calmly to her. saying all he knew. the man's stem put in – him coming in her

her saying such also.

They'll look along the road, have entered her apartment. And she makes her way back, hitchhiking with curious boys cruising in their chevrolet in the dark to the neighborhood where the living is junk.

she's stopped at a friend's who's a cop.

he'd slept but quietly she takes the .45 out of the drawer.

then she's in the dark on the path to the back yard, a vacant queasy and then wild feeling of fear.

There's a rustling in the brush with the night hanging over it. she drops and slides on the wet grass seeing the figure of the old sack lying in the chair dimly lit in the moonlight.

she isn't there. The (other) has to stifle a laugh as she's losing it — imagining.

While she's having this reverie they're moving into the backyard in the dark — and as if floating carrying jutting as if a masthead the old woman still alive as she is moving.

wriggling jutting. They haven't seen her yet.

There's no sound. She coils around lying on the grass raising and fires.

They're floating toward her, a man winged flying off apart. sagging, blasted.

tears come out on her face. Her chest is crumpled and a reflex of crying — she fires into the midst of the clump, a man caught in the fire.

they've left the sack old woman, who's lying on the grass softly weeping.

in the dark ways between her and the downy bat they're firing.

coiled partly raised on the grass firing

someone crying in pain. the tears standing on her face. her own face.

the men leave because the neighbors have called the cops. they can't be caught

She crawls to the darkened slumped sack on the grass. Holding her in her arms, the darkened frame is rattling. Gasping, the heart banging with such fear that it can be felt fluttering. faintly.

sack frame fluttering in her hands. The (other) is desperate. The woman dies. They're in front of the house, so she leaves the corpse and gets in the brush.

hitchhikes out of town. rim on the horizon and rim of cars. a car goes by and the sound of its tires on the wet highway comes back afterwards. another car and its sound comes back. it's raining.

She's lying by the road. sleeping in brush.

The man's family had died in a fire set by these men. The old rolled gun-barrel resting in his gut firing, who'd been taken out by the man – was in the cocaine with them

He had not known that.

We have the sense that children are not connected to their being.

She's sitting in a bar lighted. seated further back. man with two hooks for hands sitting in the bar – been in the war. they're friendly warm to each other saying all they know sitting at the counter.

it's flooding. in her. it's like a hose going off. flapping as it's pouring out the water. She's tired sitting there. and yet she's behind that

goes out. the vast swirl of the stars are out in the sky still.

They'd chosen as part of their crew orphans. So they had no families. And were therefore loyal only to the structure and so when there was the uprising they killed as many people as they could.

they go on as they have no other attachment.

it doesn't follow, or conversely.

have it be only (these) events and it will come out the other end of that

their work was connected to their survival – they were not feudal serfs, (whose work would not be connected to them).

as were, in this day, those who were mowed down by the orphans – and who rebelled afterward and of course, as they rebelled more of them were mowed down.[17]

looking into the high ocean from the pier these tied fishing boats were riding on it. on the mass of water. black air.

actually the newspapers in isolating events create the jewel

just go this way and
one won't be able to come back
as if they are to be sorry

What's to be sorry.

She comes to the lighted window holding her breasts, cupped in her hands as if that's going to clothe her.

there's been something out by the boats.

The man had put his stem in to her – and on her swimming around.

she was on the stem

him coming in her – swimming on her flat on her.

her flat. on the stem.

so that she comes on it. he has. after he's come and on the stem.

grey swell, rising the person's back on the hull of the boat. the back into the hull, rising on a crest in the ocean.

back into on the hull. back is on swell.

to be on it with the back.

The taking from life is the plagiarizing. So we come round again.

The orphans are afraid of reprisals and so they continue fighting. just mowing down ordinary people. opening on them in the street.

they went into hospitals and dragged people out. they fired into ambulances.

Their dictator is caught and dead. and still they continue. yet with thousands of the populace dead in a week or so from their mowing them down, they will fall.

17. is rebelling and to define it as that is to make it invisible

I used to wake up in the morning higher than a kite on my own and crash by evening. It was flesh. And yet one can perceive something by flapping

cows are swimming on the brown yellow fields

She has settled in the fishing community. A muscular man of the tied floating boats comes and asks her to protect him – it's drug smugglers, who use the coast. Coming in on the rim.

He says this in the bar – they won't let him go

he's out in the boat for days – isn't seen – which he wouldn't be anyway.

rows of the straw-covered dunes.

row of waves. light is coming over the entwined corpse sack. strewn on the sand.

seeing on the retina

flecks of sea foam are on it. it's covered in the sea foam.

mudbeds. going out on them. the wind is blowing on an inlet. corpse in the slate-black water being blown in the ripples.

She walks back. coming back on the mud flats, sand is being blown over the mudbed in a thin wave.

it's cold. she hugs her jacket. hoses of weed on the sand. in the flecks and light.

She's seeing the hull of a boat come in. rim of rose-colored light of horizon in the mass of water.

she's in it, wading. the man is in it. still alive, he's shot. the man's trunk turned over in the boat on his face

and rolls out into the water with her gliding him heavily.

holding him in her arms, the wound

have this just meet with life. no reason for it to do that.

the wind on the straw lime-colored grass on the sand.

it meets. there's no need to.

The man gets back to the town.

————————

in the boat out so that the mass of water is heaving up and black
mass of bowl is in it. There's no horizon.

The man has been in the boat for several days. He has compassion.

clouds flying over the moon or it's flying and the boat is flat in it.

in him

very golden sky one night with banks of clouds appearing to billow away
from the center though not moving and the water is under the light space.

There's a center of sky where it's light when a form is moving toward him
through the water. Moving coming on it.

They're chugging through the water. Sound of chugging comes up before
them so that he becomes calm. Four men are on the sides of the boat.

Troughs of rivulets separate the men in their boat from him whose boat is
flat in it

chugging a man holding a semi-automatic rifle stands at the side in it that
is coming in the plain of rivulets

coming in the rivulets and firing

as he's starting the motor — spray on the motor as it's starting.

outside of her
she is not in sight

Spraying chipping off the upper half of the boat.

He's lying on the deck wounded. The light of the center has vanished.
They begin to come on, boarding on the sides.

pours out firing into them lying — center gone

who fall back heavily into the ocean. He can't move to the boat's side to
see them.

Chapter 3

There is no need for this to meet.

The man flat on her – flat and swimming around with his stem in.
    her flat swimming – on the stem
    flat. and coming – after. as they're both flat and then come.

huge waves streamers go in light.
    They're driving on the mountain road, are by the mass of water. The only whale rolling its thick back heaving.
    the sole creature rolls churns
    there's another one. ahead in the sea.
    There is no relation between there not being interiority and there not being a relation between the adult and the corpse.
    there is not a relation between the adult and the corpse
    and seeing on the retina
    Her gliding the wounded muscular man heavily in the waves, he lay sack strewn on the sand for awhile unable to move. She moved nervously around him as they're out visible on the sand.
    standing. She's a small person. The man is heavy, with the shot wound in him and being dragged seeking to assist her in pulling him.
    an effluence from him
    the weight and the shot wound in him and yet seeking to assist her from in

his abdomen or belly. as an effluence that will make him light. have it be outside him.

which it is. and they're assisted by the night covering them while she's still pulling him on the path to the car.

The muscular man is drenched, cold. so that later he is really weak.

They are going to come after him. He's staying in a shed, not where he lives.

something occurring from this
seemingly

He's lying in the cold dark, his wife pressed against him.

to warm him. to keep his circulation going.

The (other) has a fear first of all with dealing with these men who're the drug contacts as that is dying. crouched in the dew drenched field.

as it gets light it's pale then intense.

again crouched in the dew drenched field at night. She hears them.

very slight sound.

fires and a flare so that it falls illuminates the field in which are five men.

the woman who's the wife running that's from the abdomen out in front

it goes dark. she retreats further firing a flare in another field. there's only the field.

Then a slight whirr in it.

the light comes very pale and cattle are standing in the field, a field which is yet further on. She's crouched in it. A cow near her hurls outside of its rear a gelatinous wet sack.

the cattle are around her. A cow on one side hurls outside of it also a gelatinous package. Her crouching lying. Another cow amongst them loosening outside of it and a gelatinous package falls from it.

They didn't find the shed.

Her client can recover and then leave the fishing community. get away, having worked for the drug contacts.

There's not meeting. There is not a relation between the adult and the corpse

between being that and dying. which isn't til a ways off.

waves with streamers manes streaking go by

figure in the illumined field from the flare running forward from the abdomen – though being inside.

abdomen projected as front of running body as if with movement.

Seeing that it is seeing it from inside out. flat.

I had to give a speech to the American Legion and didn't want to because they're reactionary. I sat in the front row and they marched up and down the aisle carrying the flag and cracking their heels together in a ceremony. They marched me up. I read my speech, apparently fast and garbled though I was unaware of it then. When the uniformed women who'd crack their heels together were going to march me on either arm to my seat, I guided them down the aisle and with gestures had them march me out the door of the hall. My mother came out after, mad though she doesn't like them either. Driving home all the way ha ha ha saying How could you do that? What went through your mind?

Driving on the ridge of the hills at night which face the Bay, the lights of the town are spread out and the lights on the Bay Bridge are mirrored in the far off dark water.

A few cars are parked on the dark ridge hanging – toward the lights. Their lights are off.

The car drives slowly so a thin light is shining from it.

Two boys go by on skate-boards down the hill in the dark.

The black form on the black air – wavering on the board.

wavers on the board and can't be seen

rain comes up on the shell of the old green chevrolet. streak from the highway and the heavy rain coming down which is a steam.

inside the old green chevrolet which is a shell humming. it drives.

the cars come up. on the ramp. glide up along the shell. water streaming from a car alongside.

a car comes up, hovering beside then gliding off to the peripheral backwash.

backwash and then gliding in it

I was on a road the driver going at a high speed amid fields people coming onto the road

> car we're in – going fast – man
> looking with sympathy,
> sensitivity – bullocks – to a dog, which had had
> its back part of body crushed – dragging itself to the
> side
> of the road – as coming from it, not from us
> – and it – a dog

the dog's back and hind part crushed and dragging itself off the road by a car that was before us – and it is in it.

the driver was bounding in the green hot countryside people crowding the road in towns.

comes up rim of people fields animals.

steps down, being caked with dirt. the sun stinging.

lightning flashing at night flickering on the horizon of the hot countryside – the dog crushed, it is in it.

the person is in it the lightning flickering across so that they raise their arms up.

the lightning flickers across in jags on the black panorama.

she's pouring – as is the dog that was crushed on the road by the car ahead.

by one that is in front of her

as leaping.

the man putting the stem in – and then as they're flat coming. they being flat do.

the man with the woman on the stem coming – him pulling comes, as if he were on it.

She drives going because of a job. Is in a disco place a bar and restaurant that is fragile.

> lit
> up old people – from green
> neon strip around – in Los Angeles – where the authorities
> had forgotten how they would look – with
> the light coming from beneath – as not revivifying
> – when – there were many of them – seated at tables

> > and
> > they all appear – very
> > old, without color, but which
> > comes from the neon
> > light and
> > not revivifying – as it – many sitting
> > at ballroom tables

They are that. Feeling joy. If it's not occurring it's not going to happen.

She walks out on the hot night. There's no space.

She passes someone she knows. They don't speak to her.

Businessmen are floating by the disco. The hobbled creature tearing its own heart.

but that's on the night. it's all right.

She gets down to the corner. people waiting in cars. A man gets out and goes in to buy a newspaper at a liquor store.

The restaurant is in precarious shape and the owner wants her to check on a buyer who'd be a partner in on it. To see if he's not into gambling and therefore into the mafia.

which the man who's the failing owner fears as he's onto some rumors and yet needs the other man's part.

the night is so warm she's a creature tearing its own heart

she's in the potential buyer's office. the window slightly open.

she has to wait as he has visitors who're in expensive suits a black limo parked outside.

She goes out to the green chevrolet. follows them for miles to a palatial canyon walled house. The black limo on the black air when it was in a hollow ahead on the road.

Had parked the chevrolet a ways back. walks to the fence to see the address.

She's holding a flashlight stepping to her car when she's yanked and slammed against her car.

the man is huge trunk muscular holding her as if she was under water in a swimming pool.

muffled sound. her struggling til she comes up to that.

he wants to know what she is doing there already has seen her registration in the car.

he's holding her up now in his arms.

she was looking for the home of an acquaintance.

When she's interviewing the man who's the potential buyer he casually says she was there that night had just walked out on having their interview in his office.

Had been to their house.

He smiles. swimming around on his stem

She says nothing.

When she gets back to the restaurant the cops are coming out and in — rather it's being messed up, there is a corpse lying as if placed gently on the bar.

The corpse who is the manager of the place is lying with a quiet gentle look on his face — which is shallow.

collapsed into itself as gentle on it

forgetting to breathe. so there is nothing in the chest.

forgetting anyone's view of oneself.

having been formed by other people

or why condescension. flat so there is struggling in it but that which it is has
no meaning.

that has formed this
has no meaning

so it's free because of that.

Oh.

she thinks. the corpse has stopped breathing and isn't going to start. goes
out into the warm night, the cop cars surrounding the restaurant.

---

inlaid. so there is no space. and therefore no getting away.

the potential buyer, who would be the partner, is calm sitting in his office.
there aren't friends and it doesn't matter.

there's a space that is suffocating the business

yet inhibited as that may be that is all there is for him.

he won't allow her to see his records. she'd say they shouldn't be partners
and not have the guy in the business. She says nothing to him. the murdered
corpse has not made space.

if one sees it that way it doesn't make any difference how one sees it

in the chevrolet following the man's red mercury

his mercury

so that he goes to Las Vegas and she's watching him gamble. the hobbled
creature tearing out its own heart — as she is.

she's not gambling. walking amidst the tables and so he's aware of her at
times. what does he care?

and so she walks out on the night feeling like so what she's not caring it isn't this

this is a job. she's pouring

and goes to the edge of town to her motel it's light morning wave of sand past there.

The next night he's gambling – and so she is amidst the tables to watch him why? They don't say he can't.

Two men come up to him at the table get in close and give it to him. just that. just come close and fire into him several times the purple spurt from him. that's there. he falls. heavily.

He's aware of her. For a moment like a breath maybe. She weeps. Standing near him who isn't that. He's not caring.

They'd just come up and shot him with the people. They don't do anything or don't remember moving.

the heavy purple coming from him.

There's a blur of the dashboard the trash in the car. weeping. what is that.

and her rolled over sleeping on the seat of the chevrolet.

She's downtown and stepping out on the sidewalk there's the freckled sandy man with light brown hair, who'd done the killing. He's a hired, contract killer. passes her.

She cannot do anything. stands on the walk. He sees her but that doesn't mean anything. flat narrow eyes

goes into a store.

In the evening, the lights are strung on the fragile facade of the desert town. the murderer is in at the tables – though not gambling.

She stands in there not gambling

is by him so that his slightly pink narrow lips quiver opening gazing past her it seems. the freckled skin is flat.

He's talking to some men standing. She's standing. and there's a fire where at first the people standing at the tables are unaware then responding and fear getting out of there. smoke and then able to see the flames. She's in there. remains there. the wet railings. char. splintered tables.

I dreamt that I had a huge circular just round bruise that was on most of my lower back and onto the buttocks.

just that.

a shiner – as if to emanate from one's back.

I can't do anything. realize that he is gone and she isn't.

The dream had been days earlier. Before this. don't know what it is.

There wasn't feeling in it. of the bruise. For it wasn't that.

The address in the canyon is an owner of two casinos in Vegas and one in Reno. Obviously the potential buyer into her client's disco who's dead was in this. and for what did they just let him play to get him in further and further?

and not the casino that had burned. the wet incinerated decor from arson. the cops say it is a takeover, it's simple they say that.

the barman disco manager of her client's going up like a flower – on the bar. as if gently laid there.

Her client comes down to Los Angeles to the funeral. They've got these birds that come forward on runners.

see. these birds that are mechanical.

that doesn't have anything to do with anything.

at the funeral very quiet. the family of the manager. on the day.

and the birds sing.

She'd like to know his mood. He's not forthcoming. Sitting there in the kitchen of the disco after in his silk grey suit rumpled. leaning forward. tired fear. she thinks. as is she.

She's in the car lying sleeping rolled. on the seat. morning, steps out where the black limo had turned on the black air coming to the house. drinks coffee from a paper cup. they know she's there. Again sleeping rolled in on the front seat. a cop comes up. move. not to come back.

The men at the gate are laughing.

She drives slowly away. gets out. urinates. What is this going to do?

calm. driving slowly and back to the motel.

She's in there. lying. gets up and washes her hair in the bowl. I don't want to kid myself. Well, you're not. The day comes apart without breaking un-rippled.

the market has created the jewel

She's at a cocktail party outdoors where these men are. just comes. is let in because there are many people coming in and out. Her client in the grey silk suit is there like a dove in the yard she sees

Flicker of surprise from him barely. And these thugs are floating else-where, glasses of drinks in hand. There is no thought. very graceful they come up telling her to leave.

driving slowly.

Man hitchhiking but he's where the cars won't stop on the highway. ele-vated highway. Cars streaming by him. She hears a thud man huddled swept.

It is not him, who's still standing hunched. Seeing on the mirror man rolled sent out from a car back.

Flashing signal, she walks back. And the man is dead sent out. from a car. He's been hit in those instants.

Yet with the cops – the coroner – says – he was dead before. They say that.

She's all alone. Well, then it doesn't matter there isn't any of that. Irrele-vantly goes to her door inside the motel room and fastens the latch across it.

Morning comes light and then intense. the parking lot. She's out on the washed freeway in Santa Monica.

They maybe had a few drops – she smiles.

The windshield crumples like a flower – falling outwards.

She's driving slowly and then accelerates. the car buffeted. there's another blast. Shot. Seeing on the mirror. the rear windshield had gone before.

the chevrolet careening – it's like it's in waves.

Tears the heart out of the car driving. A shot coming off the metal. in the light. seeing it on the mirror.

They're gone. cop car gliding

She's worn out. weeping. crumpled in the shot car. She's just drifting then. on the traffic.

> dreamed was telling him how
> much I loved him and he turned
> away saying that depended on them on
> some others' marriage

she was dependent on them, some others in the dream.

wakes. lying in brush.

Must have been lying in the street reading the sky. The two at once.

Remembered seeing a man who was saying is the water still green there? in a lake. and the woman answering him says that's not nice. And he says he's color-blind. seeing the woman walking away begin to laugh.

it comes back in

Walks by a schoolyard. Children in the court. dribbling ball. The man who's the teacher says Let's see. Let's see what you know. it comes back in.

a man's dream

he says I was on a high plateau. It was a rock-strewn desertlike terrain. I was thinking about rock walls, how the Incas cut the stones for a matched fit. They could do this if they took huge rocks and shattered them and as I looked at this big rock I saw or imagined it shattered. As I stood on this plateau, I saw a geologist or I made him to be a geologist. He came closer as they come close in dreams. So at that point, he had a pack and he said I want to show you these bees. He tore open the skin of the shape in the pack and inside was a sort of bee hive. The bees were sort of stunned. It seemed as if the bees were stunned. There was some movement. There were one or two adults like dark large bees, and there was a mass of the larvae. At that point he asked me if I wanted to eat some. I didn't find them appealing but I wasn't repulsed either. But then he drew out a large one like a lobster, or large silverfish with pincers, and he held it on its back and said these were considered a delicacy. At that, I could imagine them as a delicacy. My feelings were neutral.

as a spool. man running slowly distortedly on the highway. It is calm throughout.

There's not a relation between seeing them and the adult

There's not a relation between that and this

They just let him gamble and yet killed him because he was into them for much more than he could ever repay. maybe.

He was to get into the disco restaurant for a takeover and yet tearing his own heart out throwing himself away he couldn't

The client owner was using him as a bait there not being a relation between him and the gamblers but rather with the owner who wants her to trace him. knowing he's going to be murdered.

h￿ving created it.

She's sitting looking at the silk suit on the gambling businessman who's sitting back in his chair. Just coming in to his office.

the window is slightly open. there's no space. and she's calm as if she were a child.

Just read slowly – as inside.

he says they didn't murder him and she believes him. he's saying sipping a drink her client has had it done as burning the casino from the vantage of running the houses into each other on it.

they're on it. that means they're going to murder him. and he's maybe going to murder her out in her car or rolled from his car buffeted on the highway.

either way she leaves. She's going to his hotel room. She's working for him and he is trying to murder her. just put this directly into it. She's walking up the hall to his room.

The grey silk dove. just put this directly into it and the man rolled swept from the car. She's working for him and he was out on the highway or had people trying to murder her.

The man's seated in his room a soft light. The silk suit jacket is on the bed. there's no space and is calm.

The purple spurt from the man falling in the casino is seen on her retina.

What is the separation between information and the unfolding of phenomena?

We've invaded a country and gotten their 'leader' formerly enmeshed in our drug-soaked CIA and we've arrested him for drugs our newsmen interviewing people in the street who say to parade him through the streets.

say to execute him. anyone who does not agree is cut off by the newsmen, not allowed to speak. They merely reflect our policy. The trial jury will have to not have heard of the invasion not to have seen the news being on it will depend on their ignorance.

so the unfolding of phenomena is dependent on ignorance. and we would stop it have it come back in if we were not that.

the grey silk dove feeding back in.

and feeding back in is ignorance

and so history is calm throughout feeding back into itself. contemplating.[3]

and so experience itself is convention and we are outside of experience.

the comic book is to enable people always to be outside of experience.[4]

There is no relation between the adult and the child and they continually create action.

Actions such as getting naked on the cover of a magazine are narrative which is ostensibly inside experience and therefore rebelling

by being outside of the present convention and being experience itself.

He flies straight at her

3. *The Geographical History of America* is a work of gaiety. It is calm throughout.
4. Abbie Hoffman is seeing on the retina.

He's on her, the room in a warp of waves from the red carpet and the wall-
paper and window.

A stain of blood emerges from the shirt. such a stain is on her own shirt.

the man crumples breathing a stain on his back

He's breathing the stain

which had come from him to her and is not in her

There's a blue sky through the window

in rebelling – they define the person
rebelling as invisible to them whereas it's the reverse
it is in there – (with them) depart from them

and so seeing on the retina
and I am.[13]

Chapter 4

the little children ball dribbling and the teacher says to them. Let's see. Let's
see what you know.

some of the newspapers displayed the dead bodies killed by our troops
seeing that, and some said our president had earned his manhood by the action which supposedly led to the corpses.

there isn't a relation to the corpses. they say.

and not to be afraid of dying.

the jewel

is not to be afraid.

She fears dying. not to fear dying is the comic book.

that may be.

there isn't a relation between seeing and the action. on the retina.

and so there's being out on the highway in the old green chevrolet that was
formerly shot and streaming in it up 5.

on pitted dry barren moon roadway with shreds of tires on it from trucks.

13. This is *The Geographical History of America* – if I am in it.

the dashboard shaking gliding

with no rain coming off of it in waves clear colorless

not seeing reality as orderly is not using the mind

it's just brown countryside on all sides and the chassy of the car shaking
in it

cop had stopped a person, and checking on them over his radio they begin
to take off on their cycle. he runs and gets on the back of it riding til it has to
slow, and then takes it down sliding. they're on it

at the same time

It is not that and we are not that either.

I'm a small child, younger than the others. The kindergarten over-
crowded, the teacher lines us up and spanks with a ruler. Everyday I
wet my pants on the schoolbus coming home, unwilling to use the
bathroom at school. As an adult, not having thought of this since then
or known it, I one day suddenly 'remembered' why I'd wet my pants:
I was playing hide-and-seek with my father; the bathroom was the
headquarters. I returned from hiding and crashed thunderously into
the bathroom shouting Ollie-Ollie-oxen-free. There was my Great
Aunt Hazel on the toilet peeing. She let out a series of bloodcurdling
screams, continually screaming as I backed out into my father who'd
come to get me looking down at me sympathetically as if to say You
were caught in a trap. From this, I must of had the idea that to be
caught peeing was a terrible thing. The mind knows what it is doing
and meets itself.

Two light greyhounds running one breaks its back in the air and has to be
put to sleep. The other regrets the loss of its sister and does not eat. It does not
want to live.

says a woman.

she says the greyhound's feelings

there is no relation between using the mind—as one does in repairing
shoes. and seeing it.

Someone speaking when another begins to speak

fear that something would come from it

so he'd rather crush them than have that. than have it occur. which he could
be in. he could choose to be in it. but he chooses instead to crush them.

the heavy weight – which for him is an attraction. speaking to stop them.
It is open – as reading slowly is.

They're going to turn it back – in order to interpret it.

talking when one is talking[6]

some people mind being made fun of – but that is irrelevant.
Seeing on the retina is slow.

Very slowly trying to breathe at night. I can't breathe or have the sensation
that I can't. as if I don't have to. though after awhile remember and then have
to. and then have the feeling and the experience of not being able to as if one
could die at night when asleep simply from just not breathing. Yet I don't die
in sleep. I wonder what this is. stop and looking out the window it's raining
trying to breathe and it is being outside of experience.

This has something to do with fear maybe. and fear has no relation to the
retina.

There is not a relation between using the mind and seeing reality
Five dainty buff deer look out of the grass.
Running with them.

fear of not having lived. even if the crowd and our country is filled with us
one must not be continually getting angry. The view of that is accurate – that
it is that and so clear. so there is no relation to getting angry. as it's the same
thing.

the number of things that have happened are finite[7]

The man running only it's in the ocean the arms floating forward and then
back. That is before. The arms float forward. The legs come floating up to
the chest and then float away. He's propelled as if from in front.

6. This is trying to speak to *The Geographical History of America*.
7. One has to make a picture, reading.

The front of the body curled the legs having floated up to it and then splayed floating back flat.

Him moving flat in it – the legs having floated back.

The legs float up to the chest – wallowed floating

and then splayed legs float back flat in it

He's back flat in it

They're in the yard by the counter-window where they order food and a boy turning splashes a girl's milkshake on her. She is surrounded by her girl-friends. That is real. Her clothes are new and soiled by the milkshake she is humiliated. She attacked him shrieking, her friends beating him all shriek-ing.

They're poor. Her clothes soiled.

I dreamed last night that I was speaking to someone quite young saying I wanted to be young.

In a Safeway and people coming in the automatically opening doors. Some women emerging in, flashed on it was them. Their having been the ones who'd beaten the boy – who'd gone to the hospital. And being them at this age. Shrieking there enraged from the humiliation put on them of the set-ting. they're being sensitive to it and being in it.

the market creating the jewel
and be that completely

what is bothering you
that you had to be on the street
I had five children

Why be in the comic book. We simply are in it.

Yet we must try to be in it. I don't know how.

Girl is seen walking on the street black on the bright billowing sky.

She comes up to the (other), and then is on the other side. with the puffed illumined sky before the (other)

reading memory only
is rem

Some homeless people are by the Safeway. where they congregate.

opening tins someone has given them, as she goes out door and by them towards billowing sky.

they're sitting holding the tins

the sky appearing to move

These guys who attack her in the sense of bullying don't do that to the individual. It is to someone. The instigating bully has a way of flattering them – so that they go along with him – in order to have that.

It is not friendship with him

or to them

it's flattery which he reflects back to himself – and seeing this, supposing one sees it – it will not do anything.

they see that

or don't – and it isn't there. They're not interpreting it that way.

Then seeing it on the retina is reading memory only.

They say – who really are all right (if that is) – that to approach anyone or the stream in that manner makes no sense. not that sense is there. it isn't. and we are open.

that we are not to comment on as supposedly we're not objective on these. Whereas, they who are doing the interpreting comment on these – the objective is producing these.

Their producing these – I am and so it meets.

really they do, as I don't see this.

If one even sees it this way – is rebelling

in the desert – dog trotting emaciated on the road.

the dehydrated shrunken remains of cattle which are hung on sticks planted on the roadside as a sign pass on the desert.

Another woman – not myself – says she was riding in a van, she was getting a ride on the desert with some men who'd been in three different wars who were going fishing in Baja.

They were of different ages – are dislocated, start drinking in the early morning

the sun comes on the line

relations are functions – are in brothels. She isn't to say – yet they want feedback to know that she isn't disgusted by them.

Riding in the van on the desert

I was to give a speech – I was to say. it had been advertised, and I was in public before it. the advertising showed a combination they don't like – they didn't speak to me there. I stood in the crowd and they're not speaking.

then I was the only audience – I thought

They left a space around me when I sat down. One of the men about whom I was to speak though he does not like that came up. speaking to me, the only one who would. None of them came to it. People I didn't know came to it.

some other woman – not myself – dreams

I was looking at cut-away model of buildings. Like looking with it being downtown. One of them was my studio. I could see right inside because it was cut away. It was in a wintry place. There was ice all around the building, and the building was burning. So there was this sensation of fire and ice. And everything was going to burn.

There really is no connection between this self and exteriority that is war. and so we are free – exteriority that is going on without us

not in any
of it

we are not.

ridiculing and gang subjection is
exteriority which is not coming from us
and so it meets

The person seated alone their leaving a space around her, is pouring and
so are they – they're outside there is no relation to them.
go forward for there is no relation to them
hanging pouring for there is no need to

As there is no relation to exteriority – the women emerging in to the Safeway
who might have beaten the boy at that age, there was no commentary coming to them

there is not coming from
them then

The men opening the tins – there is no commentary, who cares

from or to them

it's invisible to them who interpret
this but if one sees that it is that
it is not so

and so this has to be serial – with it being in front.

desperation is serial
and so can't be seen by them

and so it has to be in experience that is in front.

rebelling people on crack is in front
and so unknown to them

The people who are young or older don't make it – there is not commentary on it for them
no one knows anything about it

In a jazz club the man's playing and everyone's speaking to it chiming in —
he says Pretend to be someone, as if they're not and will not be the next day.
Their faces fall. He's interpreting them back to them.

> might as well be on crack
> don't tell *me*

I realized this he's saying I'm nothing — why do they do that

> and so it is exteriority
> interpreting the inside

and so we're in the comic book because that is just inside
They can just be the jewel — they don't know it

> as the comic book is invisible to them
> for it is inside, they can be in it

Who are *they?* — their irrelevant

> their saying that we're in narrative as constructed and
> that we should be outside of that — that that is lowly.
> experience is lower class
> we'll just be mad insane and not be inside. Their saying
> that we are constructed — and they're constructing it.

Trying to reverse us and turn us inside out

Walking amidst garbage when there was a man lying in it who was
dying starving. He didn't care. I was a child. And then later walking on
an empty street with my younger sister across it who was crying afraid
to cross. There were no cars.
    An adult says to go to her because she is crying and afraid. Why
didn't the adult go to her?

The child has no relation to the adult — and so crosses the street. rebelling
is that.
    The child rebelling as completely accepted to it — that that is the mind — is
the comic book

weeping is it

I always thought that my only problem was
being controlled by them that was true.

do without knowing it
and so it meets

The ocean's coming down roaring in a great sheet not just waves. No one's
in it now. When there are people swimming or standing they are in it. A flat
plain.

subjection to gang ridicule sitting
with them who're friends
is in front

Facing a blast of light in the sky illuminating what there are immense jutting cranes on the horizon at the port—but seen from a street with small
houses as if it were a direct connection to it.

Children in the street—behind the sky—batting or playing something,
arms fly up but aren't seen directly.

Then later seeing them, those same children directly—through a fence
facing the fiery red sky with a crescent moon hanging over it.

she is not there is
outside

Seeing from a cemetery, the waves of gravestones birds singing—looking
through the fence at the children. Whose backs are seen.

They're facing toward the sky.

The men who're the thugs were moving forward through the stands of the
vegetable market and the muscles rippling arm arches backward—of the
man behind them who's beginning to move.

man holding broom handle that had stuck in the man who was moving
forward—arm arched floats forward with it.

at the same time.

They're after him. At the same time – and so there isn't time before he's running in front of them.

There's space which is communing in front

> meet them right up
> to them which is there

Flying down the slope running into their firing. Puff comes out of trees as she's in flight

anger can be as to just come to them. that comes out of the trees before her. Puff.

They're firing. Line on grass or there's grass and line.

Clearing, into clearing. Puff. in clearing.

> humiliation is immaterial then and
> so empty as separate

Line of them firing and to be up to the side of that the same as humiliation is separate. Just be in there to it the same is separate. Running and in them side. Not let that slip apart from them. As to them separate.

On sand is strewn sack corpse of seal seen in swimming on it.

tail fins strewn back behind, out. Behind it and wild grass on the rim wave swimming on it.

Puff. that's behind her. Flash of it behind. from line of trees.

> comes from line

to side as same to seal long weed bulb perforated and sack. not to have that be any thing. as up to that side is separate. the same as that, at the same time.

and the corpse sack extended swimming blossoms cups of them swaying. out ahead.

dazzling amidst cups on stalks in sheet

running in sheet
they're firing from behind running in sheet of cups blossoms
line of light horizon on sheet of swaying cups running. Burst from behind.
anger is not there is no space. I'm tired of taking this from them.
there's no space so vast sheet of cups in light
who's going into success as being that is valued and sneering at that which
is empty and in that is separate. it is even to it side separate

weeping in sheet
of cups

Having run is kneeling weeping with burst of rack
rack of sob drift out over sheet in light
as being jeering empty

there's no space then

pulp of firing which they then jeer at and so this is only empty.
has to be pulp as that is not discursive and therefore further and further
away. from them. and yet along side them in their convention. people very
successful. there.
that has been through it in the flat empty stream
doing the same thing as an event so it appears to be that is empty. And they
turn that back to be the event. To interpret that back to it. which doesn't
exist.
swirl of grass that is on that
very old man writing and keeps writing in it saying that (they) regard it as
senile. as twaddle.
that is this. flat stream is in front.

we don't see it

bird sang at night. it just sang. it's night.

I can see this is a novel. say. condescendingly.
the serial separates from it.

214

their jeering at showing one was affected but
then have to do that get into that only
of being affected as only such

If they're going to turn that back why does it matter?
out onto sheet of cups whirr
sheet of cups blowing
long moving sheet running in it out on

grove of blossoms surging
on it

the serial is just forward linear so there is not behind. it's pulp so one
doesn't know what to do. it's completely open and real. wavering. serial not
reflecting what is seen. one doesn't separate between it.

Men coming to one by lake. They're carrying chains and a crowbar the head
of the Klan.

We were trained keep talking reasoning with them; not going into the fe-
tal position I'm talking he takes my guitar and breaks it on my head. Clubbing me with the crowbar broke my wrist.

I dove into the lake. swam under deeply – he says this – with them pouring
bullets in, shooting into the lake.

I'm in the lake with they're firing and I waded up onto the other shore but
they'd come around by then.

head of the Klan came at me and this time hit my knee cap with the crowbar. I got away through the bushes tearing to get to the house.

A barrage of bullets went through the walls, were coming through – I said
on the phone to the FBI agent will you protect us? and he said I'm sorry I can't
do that we are not a protective agency, with the bullets firing into the house
we are an investigative agency. I said will you come and investigate these bullets that are between me and my civil rights and he said I'm sorry I can't do
that and rung off. I passed out waking when they're putting me into a black
hearse that the black families had found to take me to the hospital.

—in the day we were safe walking in their community because there would be a person here and there sitting on a porch along the way with a shotgun.

—I lived with a black family I could go from there but he couldn't go. He'd drive to rebuild the church that had been fired. They knew what he was doing and he was going to be living there.

—we put magic tape and a hair across the hood of the car

one morning he wakes me says the hair has been broken the car is outside by the room where his children are

we roll it down the hill with the four sticks of dynamite tied in it. I'll call (some agency) and he says You call but I know how to detach it And having done so then just drives on to the church.

—they moved me from that hospital since I was unprotected to the larger town, which was still small.

Tried to get the records, in order to press charges on the Klan for attempted murder. They were never charged. I was sent to the wrong town, 40 miles away without protection. I was told I couldn't be allowed to see the records. The FBI who're from families of the community wouldn't cooperate either. Finally I was allowed to see my own complaint. At a hearing, they asked what was I doing making trouble, who paid me to come there? They didn't care about the Klan attacking me.

we came out of the courthouse—I was with my lawyer (Where was he from? He was from Boston)—and the crowd was screaming (What were they screaming?) Nigger-lover Jew-boy. There were state troopers we said We don't know who sent you but we're glad to see you Can you take us out of town they said no we escort you only to your car. Which was around the corner—(*I* say, not him, o thanks)

and we get out of town—but two trucks come on the mirror after us pursuing—and I say to him I'm going to floor this. (I did and the car went fast.)

(That's when they were looking for the three civil rights workers. We knew they were dead the Klan had circulated their license #.)

One has a conventional surface that is constructed in conversation of others and out of it and one makes a surface to contend with that constantly yet is either destroyed in the constant attention which allows light to shine through some other inner surface (which isn't that) or one may not remember when the convention is there having come up to it.

An event is not in the person.

Chapter 4

Seeing the children directly, toward their backs who're facing the illumined sky – is seeing them when they're entirely in reverse. They're behind.

Immature in regarding this. There is not anything to see.

Depart from them.

> crowd rising coming toward one
> in a dream in which I kept trying to remember
> the line which itself would rise sweeping toward me

the line or caption itself, that was about the crowd.

I had a dream the night before last that I was going insane. I'd offered to make coffee for them for two people, and I became agonizingly confused about the loose grounds being immersed with the water. Unable to separate them. I would be using a huge pot with the grounds and water, or a small pan with burnt bubbles encrusting on the inside of the pan. He looked in the dream at me concerned, wondering. She looked at me disapproving warningly, do not be insane.

Stars dropping and crossing the full bowl of the sky. Another drops and crosses the black air. A mass of them on the bowl move. Seeing. feeding in. Stars swoop dropping and then trailing on the bowl.

Man walking on water that is shimmering. Casting line.

Men standing scattered on water. That is rippled meeting running. Line or wedge of men standing on the center casting.

Having the man's dream of the bees appearing sort of stunned and then being held up out on the plateau – not having it again. It going on at the same time – as his, is his.

says says

The man's knees jutting and then hams stretched back and then forward in the evening by the market.

Someone sleeping on the street has done so.

not being constructed is being
inside only

them

to act as if one has understanding when one doesn't. just being an imma-ture punk who is acting. so it may occur later.[8]

and so feel so relieved. that forward out in front

Calm outside of the jewel.

Leading and so don't have to know anything.

doing the same thing as an event so it appears to be that is invisible

sliding down the slope after those carried onward down it in the sedan chairs

who're condescending, jeering

slipping running after throwing cow turd them carried on ahead on the yellow slope is empty.

She is happy and wakes. The phone's ringing. The man who'd urinate in his stall – calm – is vacuuming. It sounds like he is raking the floor. in. It's a woman with a frightened wane voice who wants to hire her. Can the (other) come immediately to where she's calling from a phone booth out on the street.

Standing around a table at a party, there were women standing there. One of the women is questioning about someone of another color assuming

8. When they go for one, it is not that person. The form is on automatic pilot, as in dreams.

mocking him as if he is inferior. As if she were a society lady as she is wealthy. She thinks she is. The other women listen as she's questioning one of them.

they see it, and she may see it and is doing it. as if it also were in front.

but it isn't. and it meets.

had met this same woman another time who is speaking of jobs says did you have those jobs simply to be cool?

making a — living — and being wealthy don't meet.

and that is experience.

> this man he says to me in the difference
> between human mind and human nature I am
> just human nature that's dumb.[5]

I worked for this old woman — and I loved her, so it's producing itself. say. a servant. dependent — couldn't make the bed right. waiting on her guests and they were shocked at being the menial — so this is getting too much attention for a menial.

This is producing this

> having to be
> like them then who needs it
> there is no need

I dreamed of so-and-so older person of shining ability and we're having to turn our pockets out to be checked. He puts across the table junk from his pockets among which is a wadded condom. He doesn't care.

There's a difference between understanding it and it being this writing.

Went by city of lighted foundry in the train, the stacks pouring out smoke into the night sky. Vast lighted city with no observer. Lighted points on it rungs tiers and the center of the pouring stacks.

blackness.

woke up.

plain of short tufts, with thin patches of snow on it with the wind on it

5. *The Geographical History of America* is meeting

sometimes. so the white fog hovering over the plain before the range may be snow that's flowing in a sheet over it.

Caught sight of hobo in box car going by other train, dressed in green down vest the hands pushed deep into it, scraggly beard, pacing in the car to keep warm.

> just reflects movements enabled
> from being a hobo

clear dazzling pan that of hobo.

men bent over planting sticks in long vast field.

endless plains of soft short green grass – with no observer – with flocks of sheep on the plains, some standing and the center kneeling.

some lying strewn resting.

flock scattered grazing or walking out on vast green.

Children are standing by the way. Men are standing face out.

Groups of people standing here and there in grass. A person waves.

Waterfall on the edge that's falling right into the town – with people in small boat hanging on its edge and then cut off by train in front of the train – then lumber mill stacks and a white streak in the sky above.

I want to die in a ditch like a dog. when it's time for that to occur.

conductor pounds on glass to hobos by the side says they don't owe no bills they don't pay no bills they got beer and we don't they don't owe no income tax. Like I do. Walks up the aisle laughs.

Boy goes by on skateboard on high bridge.

> other than them where
> is what they're doing

Men on bicycles peddling blowing past warehouses ships. Cranes dangling over river from train yard.

Cross river and speed boat coming straight toward with pretty wake goes right under.

looking and not see the observer and so there isn't it

(isn't it which is looked at).[18]

She goes out and gets in the car gliding down Derby to Telegraph and along it but there is no one around.

there are shot wounds in the glass of the booth out a red smear as if an insect has been smattered in the crate.

if one says this — reading aloud — it has to be described

saying and so it is invisible to them. or seeing.

with nowhere that isn't open to run

She walks there's no one out. on one of the quiet streets there's a corpse thrown face forward into the gutter. Running toward it, sees the voluptuous corpse trussed in a tight red dress.

She turns her over. faint, she revives as if emerging from a trance. Lying there nevertheless without moving — the (other) remembers — and the wounds are barely scratches in the big woman's sides.

she's examined later — taken in the car. dragged on the walk partly on her own as if heavily drugged.

a blonde mane a painted curve for a mouth which is not saying anything from the clinic bed. nothing forms.

The (other) sits for a long time.

The painted curve as if it's making a sound to which there is no relation says they're.

they're the painted curve presses. reenters sleep.

Lying stretched out on the bed. The I.V. has been run into the woman's arm. The mane of blonde hair stretches out on the pillow in billowing waves.

The lids flickering at times. The painted curve is relaxed and slightly open then

18. either clear dazzling pan that is person or what is seen.

the crowd swimming or standing in the ocean. in it
if they imitate them they usurp us — no they don't

leading with the dreams. They lead. One can have the understanding and say it and it is not it. To have the dreams and they would just be themselves. whatever. which is the extension of this.

for this to meet

The woman found in the red dress has been in the newspapers as the affair in Washington of a senator in a matter already publicized. feeling they say. It does not seem likely he will either contact her or comment.

He does not. the (other) sits outside his house. He won't see her. His secretary is outraged speaking to her and cold as if speaking to newspeople seen as filth.

The (other) calls again from a phone booth. The woman has been overdosed and yet she is not dead.

He will see the detective. He is on vacation. This has been a messy circumstance and the woman is overwrought. She has overdosed rather than been overdosed. Oh thought it was the part of her not being dead that had affected him.

that too. there weren't any bullets remaining from the supposed attack on the booth.

how does he know. but the cops have been to him.

transparent and empty as flaccid rather than being what that is. he does not have dreams. I say doesn't dream, not simply not remembering them. So that looking into him is like seeing a pithed frog as in class. having to do that to it.

Being in the class pithing the frog.

a man's dream, which is last night
He says I dreamed this as I went to sleep, not in
waking up. People were like sea grass. They moved as
if they were sea grasses under water with the swells

and the current. The people who were as if on stems
moved as if a depiction of their speech or interactions.

to have their have pain that is
the worst to have they're have that

says a man or she says.

the populace when the repression
is removed turning on its minorities and
killing them who are within it

and so the surface of ordinary life
is calm what is that it's the same

I thought the surface of ordinary life
was not calm

so we're just out there

Climbing through the heavy straw lime grass ridge. The sand's coming in
in sheets from the ocean. It's cold. Wads of the grass brushing between her
legs in the bare part.

Going through a swatch wad of heavy grass between the legs.
on swatch. Naked part between the legs. The wind's coming in.

She returns to the clinic. She has no relation to this. Though there is a relation to the retina. There is no way to live.

The woman has not hired her yet. The woman may have created this herself or be murdered.

She has no dreams herself. it really doesn't matter because living is being
free.

this does not mirror me
and so there is no need to meet

She sits by the woman who's in the bed. Outside of Baudelaire's experience too. or in. so it's outside the end of his society. It's light and a movement
wakes her of a form in the room. She rises as it's running careening into trol-
leys in the hall to get out.

she's running gets out on the deserted barely light street

She goes back to the room. The senator is there but now sobbing weakly frightened.

The senator reduced to flaccid weeping wreck says he had sex with the woman

him putting his stem into her – and pulling it out. coming on her gently. outside of her.

he put the stem into her, jerking back. Entwined comes.

she comes with it in her

the comic book is the meeting of these.

He wasn't intending to harm his former mistress and the running man was to divert the detective.

so that the senator could simply speak to her. who was drugged.

it's believable if he believed his mistress, unhappy, had overdosed.

it is not using the mind. she goes to the address of the man who was running in the hall.

He does not seem surprised. His front door is open so that he sits behind a screen door.

we choose communing. it is not convention.

communing as convention

then it is rem
they're torn sack as if rubber

He does not move. speaking with a mechanical sonorous quality as if the voice came from under him.

He says he was hired by the senator to get her out of the room. the voice comes from under him. The screen door is locked. She rattles it gently. The man doesn't say anything else.

rebelling may be irrelevant and that is feeding in – to what?

their irrelevant

rebelling acting is taking his own life

rebelling is feeding in — calm

It is separate from the understanding of it. She goes down from the landing. There's an open court with plants. The (other) hides around the corner, in a corridor leading to the first-floor apartments.

Many hours go by. Six hours. She does not emerge nor does he. Around eight, in the darkness several men come in and walk up the stairs to the landing. They stop at his door, entering.

She is immediately roused and goes up the stairs.

The man is sitting in his same place behind the screen door. Having been cut, the screen easily moves at her touch and she steps into the room.

very close to it

The men are standing in the dark room having turned on a lamp which makes the seated man visible. The men who've just arrived seem startled at her entry.

One's hand is on the shoulder of the seated man.

He says low Bill we'll see you later. They glance at each other and leave.

———————

People are forced to be a schizophrenic, being seen as that. One mind or the other is allowed. There is not one or the other, this can't be described in this way. Yet if 'one' is seen by people, the other is invisible to them. They do this to themselves. Regarded as inferior, it must be eviscerated — yet utter loneliness is created by this very one being solely valued. By some — and so it's so confusing. There is a sense of relaxation in walking seeing the round moon which was silver and mottled hanging above some houses in the light sky. Because then I am only walking.

unless we are not experience

to be out there is to protect others. And imitating
interior and exterior movements. To protect others is

communing. But this is not true. To stop that, not having
the view of protecting others is communing. And communing
doesn't exist.[9]

The man comes out of the apartment building toward evening. He's
walking on Telegraph where she follows. In a stream of people. And they've
parted and leave a clear space.

The man darts into it a blur
at the same time her hams stretch back and forward in the evening air.

She bounds – at the same time as him[10]

He is ahead of her – her moving a leg back and forward and the other leg
back and forward

He stretches his hams forward and back – and accelerates past her meeting without touching him.

breathing the lungs are weak flaps it is outside of them

a movement forward when it is outside

then breath very deep in. then it is outside in the evening. the man has disappeared into the crowd.

She's sitting in the coffee shop early looking at the newspaper. and really not
seeing it.

or reading it

reading memory only

So there isn't a relation between the corpse and her.

She doesn't see it and it's a clear light day. she hasn't been lying in the alley
before coming in here.

Her partner calls her on the radio later when she's in the chevrolet. The
woman trussed in the red dress has wakened and checked out of the clinic.

9. Some impulses in the reader are set going because the person in the writing is doing those
maneuvers in regard to others. It is the same.
10. You stay away from them
   (as protecting)
   but I'm afraid that someone's going to die
   downtown.   (paraphrase, Joanne Kyger)

The (other) seated in the car envisions or 'hears' the click of her highheels down the clinic hall.

The man who had run down the hall is dead. And who'd run down the street from her. The (other) drives.

> there is not a relation to him
> from him

The blonde woman comes out on the street and hails a cab. in the cab. leans and has the driver stop steps out and hails another one. has that one stop after a few blocks and the partner glides up in his cab. the red dress bends and slides in sitting in the back seat and says on the mirror to take 80.

The (other) is following them not within sight yet.

> this is not being
> in anything

They're in heavy patrolled traffic and then when they're out on an empty stretch the bridge going over a stream the chopper that was hanging in the sky far back at a distance comes forward.

It comes down on them and is right over them. the shadow of the chopper is on the road in front of them.

action doesn't come out of seeing

there is not seeing on the retina

Then whirls to the side turning to make a loop and the cabby floor-boards it

to get off the bridge. the chopper is coming down again dropping as if from directly above. and they're off the bridge

as the chopper firing flak strafing coming straight on them and the cab slows. the cabby says get out

a line of flak hits the woman and the cabby on either side rolled. the cab goes up. a flaming torch in the highway.

and the woman rolled begins running the cabby calling to her.

he runs after her. The chopper heavy sagging in the air is ahead of them. It is a military helicopter.

The woman's hair is blowing. the chopper comes around back. the cabby calls to her. she hits rolling to one side face down.

the cabby rolls face down. they're in a field. chopper comes over without flak.

the cabby aims and fires toward the engine which bounce off like a nickel.

in the field of swans. the swans coming up. floating into the chopper as it's right on them. and they're taking off.

flak and the ceiling of swans

the cabby aims and fires into it the chopper swerving staggering in the swans.

and then aflame in the ceiling of swans. the woman and the cabby are running.

> they have lived. they do
> out coming
> along the street

> we do live inside

> only – and
> not inside is the jewel

almost died at night sleeping from not breathing. the breath stopping completely and then the heart madly racing to start again and waking. inside it.

looking up at the ceiling of swans – the chopper
   the cabby blowing under it
   they were meeting
   woman in the red dress sack extended blowing. flapping
   loose sack stretched out arms floating-back under ceiling
   legs floating back and forward under ceiling

man standing in scummy pool

    sack of loose skin illuminated as if rubber in light from the sky and from the pool.

    extended sack of white skin as if rubber slowly blown in light

    sack stretched blowing

It's trash and so completely the market. say.

    a rattle with no sound when I'd stopped breathing. in a shed at night with the heavy plants drooping outside. quiet. entirely inside myself. coming awake aware that it had stopped completely and on itself to start.

    on itself.

    out walking by magnolia blossoms cups and entirely inside as there is no sense of there being anything in there.

Design by David Bullen
Typeset in Mergenthaler Sabon
by Wilsted & Taylor
Printed by Maple-Vail
on acid-free paper